"Still scared, aren't you, Adams?"

"I don't know what you're talking about, Carter," Jeri retorted evenly, hiding the resentment that flared at his reference to the other time when she had fought, terrified, in his arms.

"Yes, you do," he said, his blue eyes holding hers with inexorable intensity. "You're often frightened. It shows in the shadows of your eyes when you think no one is looking. It shows in the way you hold your body, proud and distant, like a frozen snow queen, too cold to touch."

"Do I really look like that?" She could not keep from whispering the words, her hands clenched in tight fists under the table.

"Sometimes." His voice had gentled, as if he knew the anguish he had just caused her. "But not tonight," Joshua said with almost coaxing softness. "Tonight, my dear, you are unmasked, and you are all that is brave and warm and innocent. Even if you are still frightened."

Dear Reader,

June is traditionally the month of weddings, and at Silhouette Romance, wedding bells are definitely ringing! Our heroines this month will fulfill their hearts' desires with the kinds of heroes you've always dreamed of—from the dark, mysterious stranger to the lovable boy-next-door. Silhouette Romance novels *always* reflect the magic of love—sweeping you away with heartwarming, poignant stories that will move you time and time again.

In the next few months, we'll be publishing romances by many of your all-time favorites, including Diana Palmer, Brittany Young and Annette Broadrick. And, as promised, Nora Roberts begins her CALHOUN WOMEN series this month with the Silhouette Romance, *Courting Catherine*.

WRITTEN IN THE STARS is a very special event for 1991. Each month, we're proud to present a Silhouette Romance that focuses on the hero—and his astrological sign. June features one of the most enigmatic, challenging men of all—*The Gemini Man*. Our authors and editors have created this delightfully romantic series especially for you, the reader, and we'd love to hear what you think. After all, at Silhouette Romance, we take our readers' comments to heart!

Please write to us at Silhouette Romance
300 East 42nd Street
New York, NY 10017

We look forward to hearing from you!

Sincerely,

Valerie Susan Hayward
Senior Editor

ELIZABETH KRUEGER

And the Walls Came Tumbling Down

Silhouette Romance
Published by Silhouette Books New York
America's Publisher of Contemporary Romance

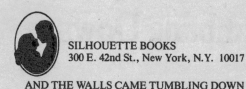

SILHOUETTE BOOKS
300 E. 42nd St., New York, N.Y. 10017

AND THE WALLS CAME TUMBLING DOWN

Books by Elizabeth Krueger

Silhouette Romance

A Saving Grace #774
And the Walls Came Tumbling Down #798

ELIZABETH KRUEGER

is the very first Silhouette author, to our knowledge, to have raised twelve children *and* developed her writing style to perfection. Perhaps her creativity has been inspired by the twelve lives she has guided and loved, or maybe her writing was her one escape from a household that, at times, must be impossibly chaotic. All we can be sure of is that we, her readers, are her true beneficiaries.

A Chicago native, Elizabeth now lives in northern Michigan.

Chapter One

A gust of frigid air followed Jeri as she pushed hard against the door to the small, dark, noisy room that constituted Bill's Tavern. Her head, neatly covered with a thick coil of dark braid, was bent downward as if she were still trying to protect herself from the January winds blowing with gale force outside. She kept her gloved hands in the pockets of her greatcoat, the hem of which nearly swept the floor with each step she took. With her practical Sorel boots feeling like dead weights around her slim ankles, she clumped her way across the room to a plain round table that stood empty in a shadowed corner, leaving puddles of snow and water in her wake.

Scarcely noticing the inevitable odor of smoke and stale beer that thickened the air, Jeri slumped into one of the scarred wooden chairs at the unoccupied table. Aching with weariness, she slowly drew off her sensible yellow leather gloves and laid them on the chair next to her. Carelessly she unfastened the top two buttons of her gray wool coat, revealing a red plaid flannel workman's shirt underneath.

A waitress appeared at her side, causing her to glance upward, revealing emerald green eyes that held an habitual expression of wariness.

"Irish coffee, Susan," she ordered in a low, tense voice.

"Sure, Jeri," the pert, red-haired waitress said sympathetically, adding in her pleasant contralto voice, "Tough night?"

"The usual," Jeri answered in cool dismissal. The waitress's eyes clouded, hurt and resentment flaring briefly at Jeri's obvious abruptness, before she turned away, heading back to the bar to fill the order.

Jeri sighed deeply. She had not meant to sound so harshly unfriendly; she must be more tired than she realized. It *had* been a hard day; a sign of its difficulty was that she had made only two of the five routine jobs on the list Giff had handed her that morning. For, along with the arctic cold that had blown in last night, came the inevitable emergency calls; people who had no heat, who needed instant furnace repair. She had handled four of those, the last of which had been for elderly Mrs. Searle.

The white-haired septuagenarian had been absolutely panicked when her house trailer furnace had quit. Poorly insulated and with no alternative source of heat except an apartment-sized kitchen stove, the small mobile home would have been deathly cold in a matter of hours. Fortunately the problem had been simple: the wind had blown out Mabel Searle's pilot. Lighting it had taken mere minutes, but Jeri had used more time teaching Mrs. Searle how to light the flame herself should the problem repeat itself. When Mrs. Searle had hesitantly asked for her bill, Jeri had replied gently, "There will be no bill, Mabel. Giff would never charge you, you know that. Just bring us some of your famous peach pie when the weather clears." Mabel Searle had blinked back tears. "Tell your uncle he's a good man," she had said. "And he'll have plenty of peach pies. You tell him, please."

Susan arrived with her Irish coffee, and Jeri accepted the tall brown mug gratefully, offering the waitress a tentative smile of apology. She took a sip, closing her eyes as the warm, drugging drink eased down her throat.

Slowly she became aware of the variety of sounds around her. Pool sticks clicked against hard plastic balls. The jukebox had Dolly Parton belting out a tune of lost love. Low male voices, indiscernible one from another in their subdued conversations, ebbed and flowed around her. It was all comfortable and very familiar. Her eyes still closed, Jeri slid her body down the chair, laying her head against its back.

"Well, well, if it isn't Jeraldine Adams, come in from the cold."

The quietly husky, familiarly mocking masculine voice caused her to stiffen involuntarily. Refusing to open her eyes, she murmured darkly, "Go away, Carter."

"You look like a frozen bear," the insidiously soft voice continued, "or maybe the abominable snowman."

The warmth of the room faded as Jeri felt an icy coldness pervade her that had nothing to do with the January weather. "Thanks but no thanks," she replied as impassively as she could.

She heard him pull up the neighboring chair, heard the light slap of her gloves as they hit the table, heard his body settling in close to hers, and knew with weary bitterness that she would soon have to leave. Opening her eyes at last, she took another swallow of her Irish coffee, gazing suspiciously at her unwanted table guest over the rim of her tall cup.

A builder by trade, Joshua Carter had to be every woman's dream man. Tall, but not too tall. Muscular, but not bulky. Blond hair that lay in incredibly neat layers. Beautiful blond eyebrows that topped the most unbelievable blue eyes ever given to man. Elegantly shaped lips that, she knew from uncomfortable observation, covered two perfect rows of snow-white teeth.

Unfortunately Jeri's uneasy familiarity with Joshua Carter's dazzling Nordic handsomeness was accompanied by her reluctant admiration for the integrity of his work. On more than one occasion over the last five years, Jeri—representing Giffon Adams Heating—had made the final adjustments to a new furnace installed in a Joshua Carter Home. While Giff had other men who worked for him do the actual installation of the heavy heating equipment, he invariably had Jeri do the concluding tests. Patient and meticulous, she would refuse to leave a job if the new furnace was not operating with precise efficiency.

Her skill, however, did not impress Joshua Carter. From the beginning of their acquaintance he had made no secret of his strongly held opinion that repairing and servicing furnaces was no occupation for a woman. Recently, though, the barbs he aimed at Jeri had become more personal in nature.

Now his cerulean eyes mocked her obvious discomfort, even as he turned toward her slightly, his broad shoulders shifting beneath an exquisitely made and obviously expensive sweater. Multicolored deer, rabbits, squirrels, and other woodland creatures wandered over the pullover's cream-colored background. Jeri had never owned an article of clothing so fine in all her life, and knew a momentary surprise that the beautiful garment could so enhance Joshua's fair masculinity.

"Been working late?" he asked, his voice deceptively mild.

She raised an eyebrow at him in silent, grudging response. He knew well enough what she had been doing. Her activities of the last few hours were all too obvious from the greasy smudges she was sure decorated her face to the dirt under her fingernails.

Unexpectedly Joshua Carter reached out a well-callused hand to gently but deliberately run his index finger along Jeri's upper lip. Jerking back slightly, she flashed him an indignantly resentful look.

"Sorry," he said, sounding more amused than repentant. He held up his finger for examination before he offered in taunting explanation, "I was just cleaning off your mustache. Whipping cream and furnace grease seemed too unusual a combination of cosmetics, even for you, Adams."

Holding her suddenly wary gaze captive, Joshua licked his cream-coated finger with derisive slowness. "Pretty sweet stuff," he said, his blue eyes holding some secret amusement. "Maybe I should have left it where it was. In time, perhaps you would have assimilated some of its...finer qualities."

She absorbed his insolent insult quietly. Silently she counted the minutes before she could gracefully leave. She should have gone straight to Giff anyway, she told herself acridly. She would certainly have done so if she had known Joshua Carter had left his usual stomping ground—wherever that was—to patronize Bill's Tavern tonight.

Successfully hiding her irritation, she reached across the table for her gloves, so carelessly dropped there by Carter just minutes earlier. Before she could grab them, however, Joshua had captured her outstretched hand and encased it in one of his own. Turning her hand so that its palm was down, he studied its surface intently. Her hand was red and chapped, with short blunt nails that were embedded with the grease and furnace oil that she worked with every day.

The movement of his thumb was feather-light over her knuckles as he said with surprising gentleness, "Not exactly a life of leisure, is it, Miss Adams?"

Quickly focusing her attention on the green light above the pool table on the other side of the room, she allowed her hand to lay passive in his, knowing from regrettable experience that the best way to react to Joshua Carter was not to react. She permitted herself a tiny dispassionate shrug, her plain wool coat shaking off droplets of melted snow as she did so, before saying to him tersely, "I'm not ashamed of my hands, Carter."

His steel-blue eyes narrowed as she forced herself to meet his stare evenly. For a moment there was silence between them. Joshua's thumb continued its back and forth motion against her knuckles as Jeri assessed the climate between them, trying to calm her rapidly rising temper. Finally she decided that she could retrieve her hand without warfare. Judging the moment carefully, trying not to give any indication of her mounting discomfort, she smoothly lifted her hand from Joshua's and let it circle her drink once more. She raised the cup to her lips; the last of the liquid burned its trail down her throat.

Joshua leaned back in his chair, deliberately fragmenting the rising tension surrounding them. He hooked one arm behind his chair back.

"I suppose you're going to run away now," he commented sardonically.

That was exactly what she had planned on doing, but the accuracy of his comment kept her rooted in her seat. Defiantly she raised her cup and caught Susan's attention. The tightly clad waitress quickly came to her table.

"Refill, please," Jeri requested tautly.

"Sure, Jeri," Susan said, her tone determinedly cheerful. The titian-haired waitress turned to Joshua, saying easily, "Hi, Carter."

"How are you, babe?" Joshua replied, smiling at Susan with disarming friendliness.

"All right." Susan grinned. "Can I get you anything?"

"Not right now," Joshua answered. "I'm just doing my duty and staying with my fellow...tradesman. Giving her a little warm company before she makes the long cold drive home."

Jeri felt true irritation invade her at last. Joshua had been less than discreet with his condescending opinions regarding her line of work, so that everyone knew of the strain between them, including Susan, who smiled briefly but with some confusion at Joshua's comment, before returning once again to the bar.

"The drive home is not cold, and your company is hardly warm," Jeri managed smoothly. "You don't have to worry about me in the slightest."

"But I do worry about you," Joshua said, his voice a silken thread of mocking solicitude. "All the time. About your frail slender body out there working until it might break. About your little feminine self toiling as hard as any man. About your snow-white skin getting rough and chapped and old before its time."

"Sure. Sure you do," Jeri said nastily.

"Someone has to worry about these things, Jeraldine," Joshua continued innocently. "You, obviously, do not. In fact, sometimes I wonder if you have any memory of being a woman at all."

With a small nod at Susan, who had obviously overheard Carter's last low taunt, Jeri accepted the fresh Irish coffee that the waitress brought. Careful this time to leave no creamy mustache, she drank with forced slowness.

Keeping her eyes trained on the wall to her right, Jeri refused to look at the golden man sitting next to her; neither did she respond to his latest gibe. Instinctively aware that cool poise was her best defense in this unsought confrontation with Joshua Carter, she was determined to finish her drink with an outwardly calm countenance.

Finally Joshua gave a disgusted growl. "All right, Mr. Ice Maiden," he said, his eyes flicking over Jeri in an all-embracing look, "When you're tired of being the man of the house, remember me. Someday you're going to wake up and find you want to be a woman, but you won't know how. When that happens, give me a call. I'll teach you what old Giff Adams has denied you all these years."

Abruptly discarding her deceptive pose of calm imperturbability, she warned sharply, "You leave Giff out of this, Joshua Carter." Meeting his disapproving stare with a fierce look of her own, she added venomously, "And when I want to discover my womanhood, I might just take you up on your invitation. I'm sure you would be the very best teacher possible. I've heard you know all the tricks."

Joshua's eyes darkened ominously, signaling that her deliberate insult had hit home. His hand snaked out to touch her face once again, this time wiping an oil smear from her cheek. "You do that, babe," he said, coldly angry. "You do that."

Then, with a movement as graceful as it was furious, Joshua stood, scraping his chair against the hard linoleum floor. His sudden movement caught the attention of a group of men sitting at a neighboring table.

"Hey, Joshua," one of them called loudly, giving his own interpretation to the abrasive tension that obviously connected the builder to Jeri. "Admit it. You've met your Jericho, and I'll lay odds that this one's walls will never come down."

Joshua's surging movement away from Jeri halted abruptly at the man's words, and the hard light in his eyes was replaced by something far more menacing. A slow, amused grin creasing his face, Joshua thoughtfully perused Jeri with minute consideration as she stared with icy calm into her oversized brown mug.

Sensing a diversion, the patrons of the tavern slowly fell silent. A low rumble of laughter sounded from a male throat, but what Jeri saw, as her eye shifted involuntarily to discover the source of derisive laughter, was Susan McDougall, standing oddly tense behind the bar, watching Jeri with concern and sympathy in her dark eyes.

The man from the neighboring table spoke again, this time to the room at large. "Well, what will the wager be?"

Quick answers came from throughout the tavern.

"Get her to a dance, Joshua!"

"Have her cook you a meal."

"No, a date! A date!"

Jeri felt freezing numbness envelop her. Only the heat of her fierce hatred for Joshua Carter warmed her soul, and she flashed her blazing eyes upward to catch him staring down at her, a peculiar expression of chagrin on his face.

"Hey, has anyone ever seen Adams in a dress?"

"That's it. A date, with Adams in a dress!"

"Well, Carter," asked the instigator of this suddenly spiteful game, "Adams in a dress is as good as anything, and a date will make it more fun. Fifty dollars says you can't do it."

Harsh laughter followed the stated wager. A slightly drunken male voice began singing in an exaggerated baritone: "Joshua fought the battle of Jeri-cho, Jeri-cho, Jeri-cho..." Another voice took up the melody, then another. Soon the entire room was filled with the sounds of men singing the old familiar spiritual.

The mood in the tavern turned taunting, cruel. Jeri didn't have many friends, it was true, but she could think of nothing she had done to any of these men to provoke this ruthless display of deliberate insensitivity.

She put her mug down, grabbed her gloves, and started to stand up, only to find Joshua's hand on her shoulder, pressing hard. Unwilling to humiliate herself further by making more of a scene, she subsided.

For a moment, Joshua stood there, his hand firm on Jeri's shoulder. Jeri stared unseeingly at the table in front of her, desperately wishing for this raucous, savage, shamefully embarrassing moment to end. It took her a moment to realize that the room was again growing silent.

"The bet's off," Joshua stated flatly, his voice cold and deep in that darkened room. "It was nothing but a poor joke, anyway. We have insulted the lady inexcusably. I want to be the first to apologize."

It took but a moment for the silence to become sheepish, apologetic. "Ah, we didn't mean nothing..."

"Sorry, Jeri."

"No hard feelings, Adams."

Just when Jeri thought her mortification was complete, that no hole on earth could be deep enough for her to hide, she heard Bob Pritchett's distinctive drawling voice saying with unmistakable sarcasm, "Jeri don't mind, do you, Adams? After all, you're man enough to take a joke. All man, in fact."

Then he sniggered.

She had not even known Pritchett was there. A relatively new employee of Giff's, Bob Pritchett had taken an instant dislike to Jeri, and he took delight in constantly needling her. She supposed, hopelessly, that the current situation was too good for him to pass up.

Joshua's hand left Jeri's shoulder. Throwing her a look that was half determination, half apology, Joshua crossed the room with hard intent to where Pritchett, a self-satisfied sneer on his swarthy face, was standing at the long bar. Pritchett was raising a nearly empty beer glass to his lips.

Joshua reached the taller, heavier man in seconds. With icy calm, he removed the glass from Pritchett's hand. The sound of its quiet thud against the wooden bar reverberated throughout the room.

Jeri, free at last of both Joshua's touch and the many pairs of eyes in that smoky room, stood, clutching her gloves.

"Apologize to Miss Adams," Joshua ordered Bob Pritchett softly.

"Like hell I will," said Pritchett, reaching angrily for his glass.

Without warning Joshua swung his fist, connecting resoundingly with Pritchett's right jaw.

Bellowing a crude oath, Bob Pritchett lunged back at Joshua, his big, meaty fist aimed straight at the shorter man's nose. Just when Jeri was sure that the nose would be broken, Joshua sidestepped calmly, and Pritchett went sprawling down on the cold, ugly floor. Taking Pritchett by the shirt at the back of his neck, Joshua hauled him up unceremoniously, then landed a blow in the larger man's abdomen, followed by a short jabbing punch that snapped Pritchett's head back. Satisfied at last, Joshua released his hold on Pritchett, and the beaten man slid slowly to the floor.

"I'm sure Miss Adams will accept your apology now," Josh said, grimly calm.

"Sorry," Bob croaked painfully from where he lay. "Sorry, Adams."

But Jeri had had enough. Moving as quickly as her thick layers of clothing would allow, walking around tables filled with gawking men, most of whom she knew only too well, she was out the door and into her service van before Joshua Carter could do anything more stupid than he already had. With a roar of the engine, she pulled out into a stormy night that seemed many times more fierce than when she had entered the tavern.

Thirty minutes later, trying hard not to think of Joshua Carter and the scene she had left behind her, Jeri was still battling the raging winter storm. Several times her van had slid dangerously; she had slowed it to a crawl. Visibility was almost nonexistent, and she could feel the force of the arctic gale shake the van as it blew both old and new snow in fast-forming drifts across the road. It was still nearly seven miles to Giff's house; at this rate it would take at least another half hour for her to get there.

Giff's house. Though she had lived there for twenty-one years, she could never think of it as home, no matter how hard she tried.

I'll teach you what old Giff Adams has denied you all these years.

Giff had already been in his forties when Jeri's father had died, and Jeri knew that most people considered Giff the rare bachelor, indeed, to commit himself to raising the orphaned daughter of his only brother. But then, to hear most people tell it, Giff was rare in so many ways—a recognized paragon of virtue in their slow, rural upstate Michigan community, where old-fashioned values were esteemed more highly than the dollars brought in by the downstate tourists. Always ready to extend a helping hand, Giff often decreased or even erased the bills for repair calls to people that he knew were struggling financially. Yes, people knew Giff

Adams and respected him for his acts, which were unfailingly generous, kind-hearted and good.

Except to me, Jeri thought bitterly. Never to me.

The van skidded again, and Jeri forced herself to concentrate on keeping the vehicle on the road. She heartily wished she had never stopped at the tavern. With the two Irish coffees in her with their mixed-up combination of stimulant and depressant, coupled with her late-night exhaustion and continuing mortification every time she thought of what had happened at Bill's Tavern, she was in no shape to be out in this weather tonight. She gripped the wheel firmly and peered out her windshield, hoping to get a glimpse of the road through the blinding snow.

Joshua Carter had no right to make an issue of her lifestyle, she thought with acrid bitterness. He had made her an object of ridicule tonight, and humilation again washed through her. She thought of Giff's employee, Bob Pritchett, lying on the barroom floor, hoarsely making his apology, and her hands clenched the steering wheel tightly.

She passed a thick stand of evergreens, grateful for the momentary lessening of wind the trees provided. In the shelter of the trees, visibility was somewhat better, and she could see enough to know that the road was not as badly drifted as she had thought. With a sigh of relief, she pressed forward.

Suddenly, with startling speed, two full-grown deer bounded from the woods and onto the road. Groaning, afraid to use her brakes, Jeri swerved to avoid hitting the frightened animals. Just when she thought she had averted an accident, a third deer, larger than the first two and with an enormous rack, left the stand of evergreens and rapidly moved to join the others on the opposite side of the road. Without thinking, Jeri jerked the van blindly to the left. She felt the animal hit the corner of the van, heard the tinkling of glass that meant her right headlight had been broken, and had a fleeting moment to breathe a quick sigh of relief that she had not hit the deer broadside, which could have resulted in a broken windshield and a van full of deer. As it was, the deer escaped without apparent injury.

Fighting the van as it bounced the buck back onto the road, Jeri tried to hold the steering wheel steady in a vain attempt to keep the vehicle moving forward, but the impact of the deer had been too great. With a sinking heart she felt the van sliding and knew that she had lost control. Like an awkward inhuman dancer, the van turned a complete circle on the slippery surface before careening toward the ditch that ran contiguous with the road. Jeri felt the big vehicle tip precariously onto its passenger side, heard the powerful crunch of metal as the hard surface met the ground, felt the giant shudder of the van as it settled with dismal finality into the ditch that bordered the road.

Breathing hard, strapped sideways in her seat by a shoulder harness pulled painfully tight, Jeri listened to the sounds of her tools and equipment falling to the side of her van. Numbly she reached out and turned off the ignition. This service van was going nowhere else tonight.

Getting a foothold on the engine well, Jeri unfastened her shoulder harness. Switching on the interior light, she carefully maneuvered her body so that she could reach the flashlight and fire extinguisher she always kept attached to the fire wall on the passenger side of the vehicle. Tucking both items into her cavernous coat pockets and pulling a ski cap over her head, she opened her door and scrambled clumsily out into the freezing winter night.

Struggling against the gusting wind that pushed and pulled at her heavy coat, Jeri trudged through the snow around her wrecked vehicle, using the flickering light of her flashlight to satisfy herself that there was no immediate danger of fire. Snow blew into her eyes until they burned and watered, and it was only with a determined effort that she forced herself to scramble back up the ditch and onto the road. She had to decide what to do next.

She was at least two miles from the nearest home, and she did not relish the thought of walking in the blinding snow. Besides, if she were walking, it might be difficult for a passing motorist to see her. But, she thought grimly, anyone coming down the road could not miss her overturned van. She decided to stay where she was.

Twenty minutes later she was questioning the wisdom of her decision. Bitterly cold, the beginnings of a debilitating fear curling tight in her stomach, she peered into the snow-darkened night. If possible, the storm had turned even nastier, and it was obvious that only the dangerous-minded would be out driving any more tonight. Regretting the time already wasted, she began to walk as quickly as the heavy snow would allow toward the nearest human habitation.

But she had not taken ten steps when she heard the rumble of a Jeep stopping at her side. Dazed, almost unbelieving that help had come, she moved swiftly, stumbling in her haste to reach the safety of the stopped vehicle. The passenger door was thrust open; she slid with nearly reverent thankfulness into its cocoonlike warmth. Before she could do more than settle her now-trembling frame into the cushioned seat, a strong hand gripped her face and turned her roughly toward the Jeep's interior light. Blinking in confusion, Jeri found herself staring into the blazing blue eyes of Joshua Carter. She closed her eyes in dismay, but Joshua had already read the open aversion that she could not hide.

Grimly, without waiting for her to speak, Joshua pulled off Jeri's hat and ran his fingers down both sides of her head. She tried to withdraw from the unexpected tenderness of his touch, but her shaking body seemed unable to heed her mental instructions.

For a moment Joshua cupped her still icy chin between his large work-roughened hands, his thumbs moving gently along her cheeks. An unfamiliar sensation shot through her; fearing he would see it, she caught her breath in a fierce effort at self-control.

She heard him breathe raggedly, then felt his hands continue downward, as he quickly and efficiently began to dispense with the buttons of her coat. Her eyes flew open. "What...what are you doing?" she asked, her tongue oddly slow and thick.

Joshua merely flicked her a hard, assessing look, his hands reaching her last button with sure intent.

"I'm all right," she protested, her voice cracking huskily. "I was wearing my seat belt. Nothing's broken."

She was powerless to stop him as his hands slid heedlessly inside her coat, making their own tactile investigation. Understanding at last that he would not stop until he knew she was unhurt, she forced herself to give no sign of the strange discomfort his touch aroused. The honest concern in his clear blue eyes was the hardest to bear of all, and she again closed her eyes.

The pounding of her heart sounded more loudly than the even rasp of Joshua's breathing, or the soft whisper of his hands against her rough clothing. She tried to take a deep calming breath, but her nostrils were filled with the sweetly pungent odor of his cologne, and suddenly she felt, just for a flicker of time, no more than the twinkling of an eye, something newly pleasurable, something extraordinarily rare, something that felt strangely like home.

She opened her eyes, blinking slowly, trying in vain to capture the moment, but it was gone so quickly that she wondered whether it had been there at all. Joshua, satisfied at last, withdrew his hands. Leaning against his steering wheel, he turned from her to look bleakly out into the snowswept night.

"I said I was all right," she said, her inexplicable confusion making her voice sound coldly resentful.

"Okay, lady. I get the hands-off message loud and clear," Joshua said, turning off the light.

He put the Jeep in gear and began to expertly maneuver his way down the snow-drifted road.

"Giff must be insane to let you out on a night like this."

She shook her head fuzzily. It must be delayed reaction to her accident that was causing her to feel so befuddled, but she could not understand Joshua's continuing antagonism toward Giff. It was, after all, not Giff's fault that the buck had leaped out at her. "Why?" she asked at last. "I've been driving in northern Michigan winters for years. I hit a deer, or I would have been to Giff's by now."

"All I know is, you're a damned waste, Jeraldine Adams."

Angry at last, she replied frigidly, "I don't need your opinion."

"I fought a man for you tonight, Adams. I have a right to an opinion."

His words, spoken with heavy emphasis, had her snapping at him bitterly. "Oh, thanks, Carter. Thank you so very much. My goodness, I don't know how I've lived all these years without you around to fight my battles for me."

The rest of the trip was accomplished in silence, made stiffly uncomfortable by the electrical tension flowing between them. The storm *was* worse, and Joshua had trouble keeping even his four-wheel-drive Jeep going through the deep drifts that covered the roads. Seeming to drive more by instinct than sight, Joshua turned onto the steep hill that led down to Giff's lakefront home. His body tensing from the effort of controlling his vehicle on the sharp decline, he guided the Jeep with careful skill to the front of Giff's long driveway.

"No way I'm going in there," Joshua said tersely. "You'll have to walk from here."

Jeri did not have to look at Joshua to know the toll driving this last half hour had taken on him. For the first time she wondered what Joshua had been doing on the county road where she had been stranded; his own home did not lie in that direction. And as long as it had taken him to deliver her safely this far, he would be more than an hour trying to get back to his house, if he could get there at all. She thought of the hill they had just come down.

Cursing the fates that had made this night one of unending torment, she turned to Joshua. "You'll never get back up that hill, even with your Jeep," she said, pleased that her voice was calm and even. "You had better come inside with me."

She saw his body take on a peculiar stillness in the dark shadows of the car, before he shrugged carelessly. "Whatever you say, Jeraldine," he said, and turned off his engine.

Chapter Two

The wind whistling and howling about them, Jeri and Joshua walked up the long driveway, past the small office building that had Giffon Adams Furnaces in large lettering on the outside, past the huge expanse of front lawn, to the large U-shaped ranch that was Giff Adams's house.

Giff had left the side porch light burning; the rest of the house was dark. Jeri breathed a sigh of relief that he had already gone to bed, knowing she had been spared at least one trial tonight: she would not have to explain about the van and Joshua Carter until tomorrow morning.

They went in through the lighted door, entering a small mudroom. Jeri switched on the light, and trying to hide from Joshua the shudders of reaction that were still coursing through her, automatically began removing her outer coverings. "You can hang your coat on that hook," she said to Joshua, motioning with her head. "Leave your boots here, too, and put your other things on this shelf."

Joshua slid her a glance of cool agreement, shrugging off his coat easily. She turned from him to place her own boots in an empty corner.

"That's some braid you have wound around your head," Joshua said, startlingly near. "How long is your hair, anyway?"

"None of your business," she answered curtly, disliking the intimacy of the small, cluttered room. "Come with me."

She led the way to the kitchen, moving quickly to put a kettle of water on the stove. Ignoring the fact that her hand shook almost uncontrollably as she filled the kettle, she tried to frame words in her head that would suitably thank Joshua Carter for coming to her rescue tonight, but all she could think of was her unreasonable resentment of the necessity for doing so.

If only she had been five minutes earlier, or five minutes later, she would have missed those deer completely. If only it had been anyone else than Joshua Carter who had finally come down that snow-drifted road. She had not wanted to see him again, ever, after that scene in the tavern. Now she was not only in his debt, she was stuck with playing host to him for the night. And if she had been weary when she first entered Bill's Tavern tonight, she was blindingly exhausted now. All she wanted to do was to curl up in her bed and go to sleep.

Sighing heavily, she turned, determined to utter the words of gratitude that were sticking like glue in her throat.

Joshua was standing in the doorway of the kitchen, all trace of mockery gone from his eyes. Slowly he surveyed the room, such a blank expression on his face that Jeri felt momentarily distracted, all thought of the conflict between them was suspended as a new, more private fear washed over her.

"Is something the matter?" she asked, doing her best to hide her nervous apprehension. "Don't you like it?"

Ever since Jeri was a young girl, she had assumed the responsibility for the running and decorating of Giff's home. It had been, through the years, one of the few pastimes that gave her real pleasure.

But not very many people had actually been in Giff's house, so she had no idea whether her concept of domestic art would be appealing to anyone but herself. Giff had certainly never said anything about the effect she had achieved after many hours of hand stenciling the kitchen floors and walls. Neither had Giff ever mentioned whether he liked the glazed corner cupboard Jeri had purchased at an auction, or the collection of early Rockingham pottery it contained.

In fact, although there was not a room in the entire house that had been untouched by Jeri's compulsive hand, she never really knew whether her results were worthy of all the time she spent. She only knew that this was one area of her life that she didn't have to show to anybody, and she had freely expressed what she never told anyone: her need for beauty, for harmony, for peace.

But it was still Giff's house. She supposed that at one time she had hoped that by making his home more beautiful, he would come to care for her, just a little.

Joshua walked to the sheer white tab curtains that covered the window over the white porcelain sink and fingered the beautiful cotton cloth thoughtfully.

"Jeraldine, did you make these curtains?"

She shrugged, trying for nonchalance.

"And you did the stenciling?"

"Surprised?" she asked, striving for lightness in her tone, a feat made more difficult by her increasing feeling that Joshua's presence here was an invasion against some privately held dream.

But he had turned away from her and was walking toward the living room. Before she could stop him, he flicked the wall switch that controlled two of the four lamps that lit the large area, and his eyes were sweeping the room.

This room, the largest in Giff's house, was done in warm earth tones, with accents of blue and green that blended with the lawn and lake in the summer. An antique dentist's chest, one of Jeri's prize finds, stood against a far wall, displaying a collection of nineteenth century children's building blocks. A truly exquisite quilt hung on one wall, hand-sewn in a wedding ring pattern. Opposite it, a wood frame set off a scene of appliquéd cows and ducks in a homely barnyard scene.

"You make the quilt, too?" Joshua queried expressionlessly.

"Come on, Carter," she said tightly, feeling strangely naked and vulnerable as she stood slightly behind him in the doorway. "I don't have that much time. I bought it." Her composure returning speedily as her anger at his intrusions grew, she turned abruptly and stalked back to the kitchen, taking the singing teapot off the stove and pouring two cups of hot water.

"I've made some tea," she said in sharp invitation.

He darkened the living room once again and took the chair opposite Jeraldine.

"Let me guess," he said in unexpectedly gentle tones, "this table is hundred-year-old oak, and these chairs are Shaker straight backs."

"You score one hundred percent," she said briefly, gulping her tea. He had yet to say whether he approved or disapproved of her work, and in the absence of any positive comment, she had to conclude that she had somehow fallen short. She tried to tell herself she could care less what Joshua Carter thought of anything she did, yet even as she framed the silent thought, she knew she lied. Joshua was a person of impeccable personal taste, and his professional reputation had been built on the beauty and quality of his workmanship. She cared, all right, far too much. She found that her desperation to be quit of Joshua's company was growing speedily. "You must be very tired," she said, transparently hopeful.

Sensing her distress, Joshua smiled sardonically. Neither glancing to the left nor the right, sipping his tea with deliberate slowness, he stared unwaveringly at Jeraldine's face.

Jeri could not remember ever being stared at. No one ever looked at her, not really, and now she found the sensation distinctly uncomfortable. What was he seeing, anyway? She knew she was nothing to look at. Giff had told her so often enough. Her eyes were too large, her nose too blunt, her lips too full.

Just when she thought she would be able to stand it no longer, Joshua stood and carried his cup over to the sink. "Well," he drawled, "where are you going to put me?"

With relief she could scarcely hide, she led him down the hall, showing him a pretty bathroom containing an old-fashioned claw foot bathtub, before opening a door on the far left. "You can sleep in here," she said.

A brightly colored quilt covered the narrow guest bed, a simple nightstand stood against one wall, and a calico cat, pieced together with fabric, hung framed on the wall. The polished hardwood floor was softened by a small wool woven rag rug laid carefully in front of the bed. Tab curtains, of a heavier fabric than those in the kitchen, draped the window.

Joshua gazed at the room impassively for a moment before glancing down the hall. "Which room does Giff use?" he asked.

"He doesn't," she replied, exhaustion rendering her unthinkingly honest. "He uses the other wing of the house. You don't have to worry about making noise, or anything."

A grim smile touched Joshua's lips as he studied Jeri assessingly. "Unfortunately I know you too well to think that's an invitation," he said.

"Well," she said, feeling suddenly gauche and childishly embarrassed, "that's good."

Shrugging imperceptibly, Joshua turned to enter his room. Jeri hesitantly touched his arm as he passed by. Stopping directly in front of her, he looked down at her inquiringly.

"Carter..." she began, as a wave of unfamiliar shyness moved through her. "Carter, why were you going down that road tonight? You weren't headed for your home at all."

He looked at her levelly. When he spoke, his voice was soft. "I think what direction I go in and what roads I travel are not any of your business, Adams."

Feeling absurdly hurt, she looked away quickly. "I just wanted to thank you, that's all," she forced out. "I was getting a little scared, out there in the storm."

Unexpectedly his hand shot out to grasp her chin, tugging her face upward. "You had reason to be afraid," Joshua said harshly. "You could have died out there, Adams. Yet you've had hardly any reaction at all. You wreck your van, stand out waiting for help God knows how long in the worst storm we've seen in years, and then you calmly invite me to tea as if we're having a summer party." He gave her head a hard shake. "Aren't you human, Jeraldine? Don't you have any feelings at all?"

Yes she did. She had plenty of feelings, and she had reacted too, was even now weak with the knowledge that she had narrowly escaped severe injury, or worse. But it was years of self-knowledge, of accepting her own differences, that had taught her to keep her emotions hidden.

"I..." she said, helplessly. "I..."

Joshua made an impatient sound deep in his throat. Before she knew what he was about, he had pulled her into the little guest room. She heard the quiet but decisive click of the door behind her and realized he had pushed the door shut with his foot.

"Carter, what are you doing?" she asked, confusion and anger battling for dominance within her.

"Going at the walls, Adams," he said, his voice a low sound of self-mockery. "Going at the walls." Then he took her face in his hands and kissed her.

He was holding her so tightly that she thought he must have expected her to resist, instead of standing absolutely still. But he didn't know her at all, not really. He didn't know that although she was twenty-four years old, this was her first kiss. He didn't know how often she had wondered what it would be like, to have a man hold her, touch her, love her. And while she knew Joshua Carter certainly didn't love her, this might be as close as she ever got to finding out what all the fuss was about. She never even thought about fighting him.

Instead she let him kiss her and waited for the trumpets to sound, for the heavens to open, for...something.

But nothing happened. Oh, she could feel the soft texture of Joshua's lips, could taste his breath in her mouth. She felt one of Joshua's big calloused hands on the skin at her nape, at the base of her thickly coiled hair. His other hand was on her face, guiding her chin and cheek and mouth. She knew she must be dead weight in his hands, but she had no idea what to do. Too late, she wished she would have fought, would have jerked away in pretended indignation...

Anything would have been better than this uncomfortable vulnerability. A slow, humiliating burn began in her stomach, and she knew she would be blushing in a moment if she did not fight to control it. She wondered if he could tell how inexperienced she was.

Abruptly Joshua let her go.

"Well," she said, blinking hard, forcing herself to be brave. "How was it?"

"How was it?" he replied, frowning at her quizzically. "How was it? Good lord, Jeraldine, you're as innocent as a newborn lamb."

He made it sound like an accusation, and she looked away from him, abruptly unable to continue the conversation. So what if she was inexperienced, she told herself in swift anger. Innocence was no crime that she knew of.

He looked at her, his eyes alight with an expression she had no idea how to interpret.

"Do you really want to know how it was?"

She didn't know what she wanted anymore, but she found herself nodding miserably.

"It was frustrating, Jeraldine. Mighty frustrating. You've got no idea—"

"Are you mad at me, Carter? I didn't ask you to kiss me."

"I'm mad all right. Mad as the Mad Hatter. But madder still at you, and that old man Giffon who let you get in this state." He laughed bitterly before continuing.

"Do you know what you look like, Jeraldine Adams? You're lovely. You've got a little heart-shaped face and the most beautiful green eyes I've ever seen. I dream about them at night, do you know that?"

Jeri shook her head, and Joshua laughed again, a short, quick sound of sardonic self-derision. "No, of course you don't. You in your work shirts two sizes too big and your jeans that are more shapeless than any jeans I've ever seen. Where *do* you buy your jeans, Jeraldine?''

Her resistance was finally returning. ''Where I buy my clothes is *my* business,'' she said. Then, feeling her humiliation deepen, she turned and opened the door.

''Oh no, you don't,'' Joshua said, pulling her around sharply to face him once again. ''I'm not done with you yet, Adams. You haven't heard it all, not by a long shot. You want to know how I feel? I feel furious every time I see your face, with your incredible skin all chapped and dried. It's not all beauty there, Jeri. It's hard work and self-denial and winter winds and January snows. And it makes me want to shake you and hold you and kiss you, until you admit to being a woman at last.''

Setting her back from him, he ran his hands down the sides of her body, stopping at the point where her hips began to flare gently. He moved his hands upward so that he was just barely touching the swell of her breasts. She was wearing a bra, and her shirt was thick, but she could still feel the touch of his hands searing her skin. He watched her steadily, and she stared back at him defiantly. Again she fought back the betraying blush, and she widened her eyes deliberately.

Finally he lowered his hands.

''You leave me alone, Joshua Carter,'' she ordered huskily. ''If it weren't such a nightmare of a snowstorm out there, I'd put you out right now. You had no right to touch me like that.''

''The true nightmare is not outside,'' Joshua said with bitter irony.

''You don't know anything,'' Jeri retorted, stung to anger at last. ''You don't know me. And I don't want to know you.''

This time he let her go when she turned and strode out of his room, shutting the door with a quiet but fiercely angry snap.

Swallowing over an unfamiliar pain in her throat, Jeri went quickly to her own room. Her trembling had returned; she was shaking uncontrollably. Unfortunately her thoughts were mimicking the actions of her body.

She had never thought that she would act the man forever. Sometime, in her long ago girlhood, she had dreamed of being beautiful, of finding her own Prince Charming. But Giff had laughed at her when she tried on makeup, made disparaging remarks about her young girlfriends, and refused to discuss any of the changes in her body. Once, when he walked in her room and saw a bra and pair of panties laid out on her bed, he had turned a bright red and exited quickly.

When he was so obviously uncomfortable with her budding feminity, she had also become uncomfortable. She had tried to be a son, albeit an adopted one, for him instead. And some of it had come easily. Never a star student, mechanical things had been simple for her. In high school she had started to tag along with Giff on his jobs. She didn't mind getting her hands dirty or smelling of fuel oil. She just liked fixing things and doing something of which Giff would approve.

And Giff was all she had. All her life she had worked for his approval until, much too late, she had realized his approval was not worth having. And now Joshua Carter was here, reminding her of all she had lost.

He had accused her of innocence. But Jeri knew that loss of innocence was not always measured in degrees of sexual experience. Instead it could be measured in the betrayal of a child's trust, in the crushed confidence of a young girl on the threshold of adulthood, in the placing of guilt too heavy to be borne on the head of a young woman hungry for life.

Jeri had not been innocent for a long time.

Chapter Three

Jeri's father had died carrying her out of the fire. He had been watching television when the blaze erupted in his upstairs bedroom. In seconds the entire upstairs was a flaming inferno. Seemingly unaware of the smoke and intense heat that surrounded him, he had rushed up the stairs to pull the small sleeping girl out of her bed and crush her head against his chest. Struggling out the front door of his home, he had collapsed to the ground, the child safe in his arms. By the time the firefighters arrived, he was already gone, his lungs filled with the deadly smoke that had denied him air for too long.

Giff had told her the story many times, and it had not taken great intelligence for Jeri to understand that Giff held her personally accountable for the death of his only brother. She had tried all her life to make it up to him. Even now, when she understood she could not possibly be responsible for what had happened twenty-one years ago, her ambivalent feelings toward her uncle continued to include both rage and despair. Rage, because Giff continued to blame her; despair, because she could never please him.

The old memories crowding her conscious mind, Jeri moved with customary quietness as she prepared Giff's breakfast. She knew that he was up—she had heard the water running in his shower shortly after she had arrived in the kitchen. She had just showered herself, and her night-black hair hung straight and damp past her hips.

If she was lucky, Joshua wouldn't awaken for another couple of hours. That would give her plenty of time to explain to Giff about the accident and about Joshua Carter spending the night in his house.

She was conscious of an unwelcome sensation writhing uncomfortably in the pit of her stomach. She would, of course, have to tell Giff about the fight between Joshua and Bob Pritchett. *That* news would be all over the countryside before the day was over. Since it involved one of Giff's employees, she supposed that it was only right that he heard it from her.

Jeri started the drip coffeemaker, put some sausage in the frying pan, and mixed a half gallon of frozen orange juice. Pulling out Giff's favorite boxed cereal from the cupboard and a milk jug from the refrigerator, she laid a neat place for him at the kitchen table. Only then did she pour a cup of coffee for herself. Wishing uneasily that her conversation with Giff was already over, she carried her coffee to the table and sat down to wait.

She was on her second cup when Giff entered. In his late sixties, Giff had aged little since Jeri was a child. His hair, still a rich dark chestnut in color, was slicked back in a style she was sure he had not changed since he himself was young. Always neat and well-groomed, today Giff looked almost dapper in his navy slacks, professionally pressed sky blue shirt, and his navy and white bow tie. A small man, Giff stood little taller than Jeri, but she knew people rarely noticed Giff's height. His ready smile, his intelligently friendly brown eyes, and his firm handshake were usually all anyone needed before they called him friend.

Which was why she found it puzzling that Joshua Carter's antipathy to her uncle had been so instantaneous. From their first meeting over five years ago, Joshua had disliked Giffon Adams.

Joshua had been the new man in town at the time. Originally from Detroit, the lakefront vacation home he had been building had been commissioned by one of his clients from the city. Giff had won the bid on the furnace.

Jeri had been in Giff's office when Joshua Carter had come to see him about finalizing the terms of the heating contract, which so far had been communicated solely by letter. Giff had risen automatically from his desk to walk around and shake the younger man's hand. As the two men's hands clasped together, their eyes meeting in mutual appraisal, Jeri had intuitively sensed Joshua's immediate, if unexplainable, dislike of the older man.

It had puzzled her then, this immediate antipathy for someone just met, just as Joshua's continuing animosity toward Giff puzzled her still, especially as he could find no fault with Giff's work.

Inevitably Giff had eventually become aware of Joshua's silent contempt, yet he continued to bid work on Carter Homes, and Joshua continued to give him contracts. To Jeri, it was an inexplicable state of affairs.

Shaking her head to rid herself of her confusing thoughts, she greeted Giff briefly.

"Good morning, Jeraldine." Giff poured himself some cereal in the bowl Jeri had provided, carefully spooning a single teaspoon of sugar on top before adding his milk. "That sausage smells good."

Automatically, Jeri rose to lift the sausage out of the pan and onto a plate already spread with paper toweling. She laid the plate at Giff's side.

"Late night last night?" Giff asked.

"Afraid so. I didn't finish at Mabel Searle's until nearly nine."

Giff nodded. "Tell me about your other jobs."

As Giff finished eating, Jeri described to him the work she had done the previous day. Though Giff said little, she knew he was listening intently. In years past, Giff would point out to her things she could have done better, ways she could have been more efficient. Now she was proficient enough in her work that no criticism was necessary, yet she still provided him with the daily recitation.

When she finished, Giff pointed with his fork to the plate of sausages.

"Planning on eating some of these yourself?" he asked dryly.

She rubbed suddenly damp hands on her jeans, experiencing an unusual foreboding at the news she must impart. "Not exactly," she replied, "I cooked more because... well, I..." Her stumbling delivery caused Giff to look at her questioningly, and she took a deep breath before plunging on gracelessly. "I'm afraid we have a house guest, Giff. I...I wrecked my van last night. I...Joshua Carter came by and gave me a lift back here, only then the storm was so bad, it was obvious he might never get to his own home, so I invited him to stay." She discovered she was wringing her hands apprehensively.

Giff slowly lowered his fork, then fastidiously cleaned his face with the napkin Jeri had provided.

"You wrecked your service van?" he asked, his voice quietly incredulous.

She nodded unhappily. "Yes, and it's probably totaled. I hit a deer, and with driving conditions the way they were, I'm afraid I lost control and—"

Giff's low voice cut in sharply. "And you invited Joshua Carter to spend the night? Here?" He looked at her with absolute disbelief. "In my house?"

"What else was I to do, Giff?" Jeri asked, forcing herself to speak reasonably. "My van had tipped. I had waited long enough for someone to come by that I was close to freezing. Should I have refused his help?"

Giff looked at her with cold distaste, and she realized for the first time the depth of his anger. Years of habit making her more sensitive to his moods than her own, she immediately tried to placate him.

"I'm sorry, Giff," she said, her voice a pleading whisper.

Glancing away from her, Giff began to drink his coffee. When he spoke again, his voice was laced with barely concealed irritation. "I must say I'm disappointed in you, Jeraldine. You've been driving these roads long enough to know to watch out for deer."

Holding her hands in a tight knot on her lap, Jeraldine knew better than to try to explain how it had been. How could she explain that the storm outside had been no worse than the storm in her soul after leaving Bill's Tavern? Instinctively she knew Giff wouldn't understand any of it. Besides, even the best of drivers sometimes ran into deer— the woodland animals were dangerously unpredictable. She remained silent.

Giff continued to drink his coffee, and she knew he was struggling to control his temper, that he would not speak again until he could do so calmly. His self-control had always been a marvel to her. It was one trait she admired so much she consciously tried to emulate it.

"Well." He stood up and walked to her side, laying a heavy hand on her shoulder. "What's done is done. I suppose there was nothing you could do to prevent it." His quiet tone held just a shade of continued condemnation. "I'll call the insurance company and a tow truck."

Feeling unexpectedly wretched, Jeri rose to clean the leftover contents of Giff's breakfast and her own coffee off the table. Turning, she caught sight of Joshua Carter, standing half-hidden in the shadow of the kitchen doorway. His fiercely burning eyes held her momentarily motionless; she had an almost frightening impression of terrible anger held in check by hard-won control.

Straightening from his slouched position against the wall, he gave her an almost imperceptible nod before he spoke to Giffon Adams, his words a softly arrogant challenge, "Don't you think you ought to ask her if she was hurt, old man?" His tone changed to studied scorn as his voice grew softer still. "Or don't you care?"

Jeri's breath caught as Giff's head shot up at the sound of Carter's voice. Swiftly turning away from Joshua, she walked uneasily to the sink to stack the dirty dishes.

Giff remained absolutely still in his position behind the chair Jeri had just vacated. Recovering quickly from his first shock, the older man smiled slightly and slowly brought his hand to the back of the chair, rubbing his fingers caressingly along its smooth wooden surface. His expression unreadable, Giff met Joshua's blazingly blue eyes steadily.

"I'm sure Jeraldine would have told me if she had been injured." Giff's mildly reproving words were oddly jarring in the suddenly hostile atmosphere Joshua's words had created.

"Would she? What comfort would she receive if she had?" Joshua's low voice cut like seasoned steel.

For a brief second, stark hatred shone bright in Giff's unyielding brown eyes. Then he walked to where Jeri was standing, her back to the sink, dazed confusion reflected in her stunned expression. Seemingly unaware of her discomfort, Giff slipped an arm around Jeri's waist. "Of course she would have told me," he said calmly. "Wouldn't you, my dear?"

"Sure, Giff." The wooden response was all she could manage, for her chest was constricting painfully over sudden ambiguities she could not quite grasp. "Sure, I would have told you."

She found Giff's answering smile curiously triumphant as he said with pointed emphasis to the fair man standing tall and still in the doorway of the room, "There. You see? But we appreciate your . . . concern, even if it is misguided."

Inexplicably ashamed, Jeri pulled away from Giff's surrounding arm. Silently she began to lay a place for Joshua at the table, much as she had done for Giff earlier.

"Don't," Joshua said, stepping with quick urgency into the kitchen. He laid a gentle hand on Jeri's arm. She remembered irrelevantly that Joshua's touch was usually gentle, even when his voice and eyes were giving a different message. "You don't have to do this for me," he continued. She could hear an undercurrent of anger still flowing in his voice.

"That's right," Giff agreed with a sneer, and Jeri was surprised to hear the open antagonism. Giff's wrath must have been inflamed indeed to cause him to lose so much control. "Carter is welcome to breakfast, of course. But I'm sure he doesn't find it necessary for you to feed him. I need you at the office, Jeraldine. You can come back here later to clean up."

Joshua's hand was still on her arm, and she glanced up to find him watching her with an odd mixture of understanding and challenge. "I meant you don't have to serve me, or clean up after me," Joshua said quietly, locking her eyes with his. "But I would be pleased to have your company while I eat."

She began to tremble. She knew Joshua could feel it; his hold on her arm tightened imperceptibly. She felt strength in his fingers; she sensed he was giving comfort she had not even realized she needed.

Giff, standing by the counter, watched her unwaveringly. Sensing some impending disaster, her stomach churned in rebellious response to undertones she was at a loss to understand. Unfamiliar sensations of fear and anguish washed through her; a separate internal voice silently taunted her for overreacting to what was simply intense dislike between the two men standing there.

Gradually she again became aware of Joshua's hand upon her lower arm. With compelling clarity, she understood that Joshua was willing her to be strong, as if she was being fortified for battle. Fierce energy was flowing into her from his deceptively gentle touch. Her eyes closed briefly as she focused on the feel of his fingers against her skin.

"I'll stay with Joshua," she said in a voice that she hardly recognized as her own. "He brought me home last night. I'll stay and keep him company now."

A black light of fury appeared in Giff's dark eyes, only to disappear as he shrugged easily. "All right, my dear. Just don't be late." His eyes moved to meet Joshua Carter's. "As I said, you're welcome to breakfast. But the snowplows will be out soon. You shouldn't have to stay too much longer." Giff stared at the hand Joshua still had clasped around Jeri's lower arm. Embarrassed, Jeri moved away from the blond man, pulling her arm free as she did so. Giff smiled, an obviously forced attempt that failed to reach his eyes. "Eight o'clock, Jeraldine.'' Then, with an almost malevolent glare at Joshua, Giff pulled on his coat and went out the door.

More shaken than she wanted to admit, Jeri turned to pull the milk back out of the refrigerator.

"I told you not to serve me."

Joshua's tone sounded smugly triumphant to her, and she stiffened. She hadn't understood exactly what Giff and Joshua had been arguing about, but she knew she had been placed squarely in the middle of some nasty game of tug-of-war between them. She had chosen to stay with Joshua, but she wondered now who had actually made that decision. Too late she remembered she had yet to tell Giff about the scene in the bar.

Abruptly she slammed the refrigerator door, swinging around jerkily to face Joshua. "So do it yourself," she spat out rudely. She walked quickly to the sink and began running water for the dishes.

"I suppose all this is worth it," Joshua's voice sounded from her right shoulder, "for a chance to see you with your hair down."

Her hands stilled in the dishwater. She had forgotten about her hair. She never thought about how she looked when she was with Giff, and the tension of the previous moments had driven all thought of herself out of her mind.

Keeping her back to Joshua, she raised her hand self-consciously to the hair that hung loose and shining over her shoulders.

"I'll just go and braid it . . ." she began.

"No," he said, his voice low and quiet in the boiling atmosphere Giff had left behind him. She felt his hand on her head, felt him lift a heavy lock off her neck.

She held herself very, very still. For years only Giff had seen her with her hair down, no one else. She felt suddenly vulnerable and terribly afraid.

"I really should braid it," she whispered. "Otherwise it will get in my way when I work."

"It's still wet, Jeraldine. Do you usually braid it when it's this wet?"

She shook her head, unable to speak.

"Then leave it, just for a little while. Just until it dries a little more."

If only she could think of something to say. But she never knew what to say or how to act around Joshua Carter. She was overwhelmingly conscious of his hand continuing to caress her head lightly, of his voice speaking as soothingly as if she were a wild animal he was trying to tame, of his body standing only inches from hers.

She should turn around, should move away from him. Maybe she should laugh lightly, make some kind of joke. But she could not. All she could do was stand absolutely still, her head down, her hands in dishwater, as he continued to stroke her hair.

"Thou art as a garden that hath no water," he quoted softly, his voice rich and melodious and full of knowledge. "But thy desert shall rejoice, and shall blossom...like a rose." His hands were on her shoulders, and he pulled her back against his chest. She could feel his head bend toward her, heard him breathe deeply as he inhaled the fragrance of her still-damp hair.

Once again she began to tremble. His words and touch moved her, far more than did his kiss of the past night. She felt again that fleeting sensation of longing, of coming home, that she had experienced when he had examined her in his Jeep.

She tried to speak. "I...you...I..." Her trembling increased, as did her fear. Desperately she tried to remember all the reasons she had to dislike Joshua Carter. She was far too vulnerable, too exposed. What was he doing to her? Just minutes ago she had been furious with him. His arms moved to encircle her, and he slowly drew her away from the sink. She heard him laugh huskily before he turned her in his arms. Growing more panicked by the second, she began to struggle against his hold.

"Whoa," he said, surprised at the force of her sudden action. "Whoa." She felt the strength of his arms harden to iron as her movements grew wilder. Her eyes flaring in alarm, she shook her head violently against the gentle persuasion of his tone, the tenderness in his eyes. Her hair swung around them both, tangling against his neck and catching on his fingers.

"Adams," he said. "Stop."

She could not. It was too much, this awful vulnerability on top of everything else she had experienced in the last twelve hours. It was as if some invisible chain that kept her bound and sane had been forcibly snapped. She was beyond stopping.

"Let me go!" she cried in bitter anguish, twisting in his arms as she tried to free herself from his now vicelike grip. "Let me go! I hate it when you touch me! I hate it when you talk to me!"

"Adams, it's all right," Joshua said quietly, ignoring her harsh, terrified words. One strong hand forced her head against his chest. "You're scared, that's all. It's okay to be scared. Hold still. I'll let you go as soon as you hold still."

Still she struggled against him, her body moving convulsively in her near-hysterical efforts to free herself of his touch. Like bands of steel, his arms held her close against his muscular frame, giving her no freedom to strike out or twist away.

"I won't hurt you, Jeraldine," he said. "I promise I won't hurt you. Just hold still, and I'll let you go."

How long she fought against him, instinctively trying to run from some hidden danger she did not yet understand, she did not know. It seemed an eternity before she could hear his low voice talking to her, soothing her, before his hands and arms felt like more than prison bands around her body. But she quieted at last, turning her face away from his sweater so she could gulp in air. Great shudders continued to shake her as she stood momentarily passive in Joshua's arms. One of his hands began to move comfortingly up and down her back.

"You said you would let me go." Her voice was a mere whisper.

He loosened his hold immediately, and she knew she was free to step away. Yet, appallingly, it took all of her remaining will to do so. Moving with awkward clumsiness, she walked the three steps to the kitchen table and sank weakly into a chair. Only then did she have the courage to look at Joshua Carter.

He was leaning against the counter, his arms folded over his chest, watching her expressionlessly.

Her first thought was that she probably owed him some sort of explanation, but she could think of none that would explain her total loss of control. She had obviously overreacted; she would give practically anything to erase the last few minutes of her life. She had never responded like that before to anyone, and with deep shame washing through her, she knew she had made an absolute fool of herself. She twisted her hands together and looked away.

"Well," she said, striving for lightness in her tone. "You will probably want to leave now."

He said nothing.

"I have things to do, too. I have to clean up here and braid my hair and get over to Giff's office before he—"

"What has that bastard done to you to make you so frightened?" Joshua's voice cut through her pretense, once again laying open the soft underbelly of her soul.

Her hands clenched as she stood shakily. "Lay off of Giff," she said, finding strength in her anger. "My problems are my own, can't you see that? Giff had nothing to do with this."

"All right then. Tell me this—is it just my touch that sends you into hysterics, or does that happen with everyone?"

Everyone? Who else did he think she allowed to hold and pet her? "Just you," she said defiantly. "Just you, Carter."

"So why didn't you struggle when I kissed you last night?" he threw the challenge back at her.

"I wanted to see what it felt like," she admitted with brutal honesty. "No one had ever kissed me before, and I was curious."

Then, because he had hurt her in ways she did not yet understand, she struck out at him foolishly. "I must say, it was rather a disappointment. Kissing is obviously a vastly overrated pastime. It was not an experience I'd like to repeat at all."

His eyes shot blue-white flames of anger at her. "That kiss was nothing, Jeraldine. You know nothing, not about kissing, not about yourself, not about me, and certainly not about Giffon Adams."

She shook her head in hot denial, her hair flowing around her body like a shield.

"You're beautiful, do you know that?" Joshua asked, his voice low and burning. Then he laughed harshly. "But of course you don't. And if you did, you would still deny it, wouldn't you? You deny everything," he continued mercilessly. "You deny your own experience, you deny your own fear, you deny your own womanhood. What happened to you, Adams? Didn't Giffon know how to handle it when you started turning womanly on him?''

Teeth clenched against some hidden pain, she swung her arm blindly. Her hand shot out, connected with his face, hard. His fair complexion reddened with the force of her blow.

Jeri stared at Joshua in shock. She had never hit anyone in her life. She had always been so careful, so self-controlled. Since childhood, it had been a kind of game with her, to see how well she could hide her feelings from those around her.

But she had no more time to wonder at her own action, as Joshua's arm stretched out in quick retaliation. He grasped a handful of her long, black hair in a tight fist, as his other hand held her chin with punishing firmness.

''You want to see what a real kiss feels like?'' he asked harshly. Feeling panic well within her once again, she tried to shake her head, only to find movement impossible while his hands held her captive. Helpless, she watched as he lowered his lips to hers.

Determined not to fight him again, she kept her eyes wide open as his lips moved against her own. She looked at him steadily, calling on years of habit and training to help keep her most private thoughts and fears at bay.

As if from a great distance, she noticed that dark brown hairs were scattered throughout Joshua's Scandinavian blondness. She saw a pulsebeat at his temple; she observed that his skin was smooth and tight, that his lashes were long and fine.

He really was a most luminous man. She closed her eyes against him.

It was a mistake to close her eyes. For it was then that she first began to understand that this kiss was totally different than the one she had received last night. She was weaker, not herself at all, no longer a match for Joshua's arrogant determination. It was as if she had slipped on dangerous ground, was even now falling helplessly to some unknown, yet inevitable, destination.

And then, slowly...slowly...she began to feel. She felt first the texture of his lips, not moist, not dry, but firm and surprisingly gentle.

She felt his hands, no longer holding her with angry force. One hand was against her back, pinning her hair under it, while the other remained at her cheek, stroking, stroking. He had somehow moved her so that she was standing against the kitchen counter; she could feel it digging into her ribs.

She began to feel herself, her own body, in ways long prohibited. She felt herself soften, swell, gain a new pliancy.

She felt Joshua's tongue scrape against her lips.

He wanted her to open her mouth. She knew enough to know that. You couldn't live in this century and not know what that tongue moving across closed lips meant. She'd read some books, seen some television, gone to some movies, in her twenty-four years. Yes, she knew what he was asking.

She had long ago given up her dreams of true love, of home and marriage and children. She knew she wasn't yet old, but some things are understood early. No one ever looked at her as a man looks at a woman, and she'd had no training in the softer, more feminine arts. She had been sure that she would never be the recipient of male passion.

So her reaction to that question upon her lips was one of sheer surprise that Joshua was even asking it, especially after she had made such a fool of herself just minutes ago.

But if he was asking, he was also giving—experience and knowledge and understanding. This might be her only chance to grasp at the slender thread.

She parted her lips and shyly, inexpertly, began to kiss him back.

Without pause of surprise or victory, he brought both his hands to encircle her face and leaned his body into hers. She had to clutch his arms to hold herself upright.

She began to feel a heaviness in her lower limbs, combined with an extraordinary weightlessness everywhere else. The world started to spin in a slow-moving circle, and she felt herself yielding, her body a new form of willing plasticity. She heard a moan and knew it came from her own throat.

She felt Joshua's mouth leave hers, felt his warm, sweet breath on her lips. "Ah, Jeraldine, you're not afraid now, are you?" he murmured. "And you're not hiding either. I've waited a long time to see you like this." She looked at him questioningly, disbelieving the husky longing in his voice.

"What in burning hell is going on here?" Unexpectedly Giff had returned to the house, and now his hot, furious voice filled the room. "Damn you, Carter, get your filthy hands off my girl!"

Joshua half turned, shielding Jeri from Giff's fierce wrath. His eyes raking her face, he absorbed the stunned expression in her confused green eyes; her mouth, swollen and reddened, quivered still. Deliberately he brushed her lips with his thumb. "Beautiful," he murmured, before he swung around almost leisurely to face Giff.

"Since when did she become your girl, Giff? You're her uncle and guardian, remember?" His words fell like a gauntlet into the room.

Giff's face was pale, his hands were clutching and un-
clutching themselves in sharp, spasmodic movements.

"Why are you hiding her, Giffon?" Joshua's voice was
implacable, his eyes mocking the older man contemp-
tuously. "Why do you insist that she deny herself? If you
can't have her, nobody can? Is that what you think?"

"You bastard," Giff said, his voice full of malevolent
hatred. "You filthy..." Words failed him, and he made a
fist and shook it at Joshua. "If I were a younger man I
would—"

"You would what?" Joshua taunted. "Take me on? And
for what? For speaking the truth? You're ruining her life,
Giffon. You've got her hiding her womanhood behind
greasy fingernails and your cast-off workshirts. She doesn't
know who she is. She doesn't know what she is. You've
taught her to work and drink and swear with the best of us,
but she's no man to pal around with. And it wasn't a man I
was kissing just now."

Giff's face grew red, redder than Jeri had ever seen it.
Frightened, she moved away from Joshua's protection.

"Giff," she said, worry coloring her voice. "Giff, calm
down, *please*. You're going to give yourself a heart attack,
or something. Please calm down, Giff."

Giff turned his accusing gaze on her. "I'm going to give
myself..." He sputtered angrily, rocking back and forth on
his leather heels. "I'm going to..." He pointed a condemning finger at her. "You are the one making me... It's
you behaving like a tramp in my house!"

For a moment the three of them stood there in a frozen
tableau, the dreadfully ugly word stunning them all with its
hideous implications.

She felt Joshua stiffen threateningly behind her and knew
she would have to act quickly to prevent further disaster. "It
was only a kiss," she said slowly, thrusting aside her own

pain, burying the knowledge of Giff's twisted anger. *Your mother was a tramp,* he had told her, before she was old enough to understand what the word meant.

She continued to watch his color carefully. "I'm twenty-four, Giff. I guess I can kiss somebody if I want to."

"Not in my house, you can't. I took you in. I raised you. I taught you…things. I have a right to say what you can and can't do in my house."

The color drained from Jeri's face. He was right, but never had he said the words so plainly. Her arms went around a stomach suddenly tense and painful with shame. He *had* given her so much, the best he knew how. If he had not given her a home, where would she be now? She owed him more than she could ever repay.

"I'm sorry, Giff," she said, her voice a mere whisper. "I'm so sorry. You're right, of course. It won't happen again."

"In this house," Joshua corrected tersely. She was surprised to find his hand resting possessively against her back.

"What?" Jeri asked blankly.

"It won't happen again in this house. What happened between you and me was true, Jeraldine. But there is no truth in this house."

"Are you going to let him stand there and insult me, Jeraldine?" Giff demanded harshly.

No. No, she wasn't. Giff had surely been as good to her as he was capable of being. And now it was too late for recriminations. The past was written in concrete; it could not be changed. Joshua was only stirring things up with his smug, self-righteous comments. One kiss did not give him the right to say such horrible things, to be so angry. He had no say over her life whatsoever.

"You had better go now, Carter," she said, her voice rough with her new-found indignation. "Giff's right. You're being unforgivably insulting. And for what? Because I wanted to find out what a kiss tasted like? I told you I would come to you when I wanted to know. So I found out. But I don't want to know anymore. I don't want to find anything else out, even from such an excellent teacher as you.''

Joshua was rigid in his fury, his eyes blue pinpoints of fierce derision. But still his voice remained softly persuasive. ''That's not how it was at all, Jeraldine,'' he said slowly, deliberately. ''And you know it. But I suppose you're more comfortable lying to yourself than living with the truth. You've been doing it long enough.''

Then, as if making a conscious decision, he relaxed, his body easing into naturalness, his eyes hooded behind a bright mocking gaze. ''All right, babe,'' he said, one long finger stroking Jeri's cheek. ''All right. I'll leave, since you're sure that's what you want.'' He went to the mud-room, and after gathering his things, returned to the kitchen to sit in a chair before putting his boots on. Jeri remained standing against the counter watching Joshua, unaware that Giff was also still as a statue, watching her.

Unhurried, Joshua pulled on his boots. Slowly he slipped his arms into his coat. Taking his time, he drew his hat down over his ears. When he was finished, without once looking at Giffon Adams, he sauntered over to where Jeri was standing bleak and pale, her arms still wrapped around her waist. He rubbed his thumb directly under her right eye, gently. Then he stooped and planted a kiss of soft possession on her lips.

Uncaring of the older man standing dark as a shadow in the doorway, Joshua murmured, ''You're mine, my Jericho.''

His hand reached out to stroke her long, black hair. As if he knew he could take all the time in the world, he reached behind Jeri to pick up some kitchen shears lying on the counter behind her. Before she knew what he was about, he had raised her great mass of hair to clip an underlock free. Looking steadily into her eyes, he twisted the long strand of hair round and round his finger, until he could slip it off and drop it like a tiny spiral into the palm of his hand. Opening his coat, he slipped the lock of hair into his inside left coat pocket.

"Just a memento, Jeraldine," he said. "To help me remember what you look like when your walls are down."

Then he was gone, out into the snowy landscape. And she felt like a true traitor at the thought, but it seemed as if he took the only spark of warmth Giff's house had ever known out there in the snow with him.

Chapter Four

Her mother had been a nightclub singer. Daniel Adams had just left the Air Force when he met her, and he had fallen hard. He was starting a career in real estate in Chicago and had asked the green-eyed woman to be his wife.

But she had put him off and eventually left town without even telling him she was going. Months later she appeared on his doorstep, a small bundle of life in her arms. The infant girl was his, she told him. He could either take it, or she would turn it over to the state.

Daniel chose to take the child, even though he later confided to his brother Giffon that he could never really be sure that he was the father. His disenchantment with his former lover had been complete, and Giff had kept that memory alive long after Daniel's death.

Why? Jeri asked silently, reviewing the story in her mind. Why was it so important that I know my mother abandoned me? Why couldn't I feel loved, just a little? Did you know what you were doing, Giff, when you were telling me these stories?

She spent most of that day avoiding her uncle. It wasn't hard to do, as long as she didn't walk the short distance to the office where he was sure to spend most of his time. She cleaned the house, did some extra baking, caught up the laundry. Later, she used the pickup Giff had given to her on her sixteenth birthday to drive down to the wrecked van. A specified time had been set for her to meet both a policeman and a tow truck there.

The sight of the large vehicle, tipped drunkenly along the side of the road, had her trembling once again. How easy it would have been to have been killed last night; it was truly a miracle she had escaped without serious injury. Swinging out of her pickup, she walked slowly around the now desolate van.

The entire passenger side was smashed in; how she had recovered her flashlight and fire extinguisher she had no idea. The wheels of the driver's side hung suspended in the air. She realized she had had to drop several feet last night when she crawled out her door. Walking around to the rear doors, she was able, with difficulty, to jerk one open. For a long moment she stood staring at the ruined interior of her service van.

Her toolbox had come open during its flight across the side of the van—tools were everywhere. Burner nozzles, electrodes, replacement filters, all were strewn in a heap that extended the length of the vehicle. The case containing her combustion tester had also become unfastened—a thousand dollars' worth of pieces lay mixed in the pile, which resembled nothing more than a wasted junk heap. Pervading everything was the smell of spilled fuel oil. She caught sight of the trashed coffee can that had been full of the stuff, a leftover remnant of one of yesterday's service calls.

Closing the rear door with unnecessary force, she returned to sit, numb, in her pickup. Pulling off her gloves, she looked at her fingers as she moved them experimentally. She wiggled her toes in her boots. She listened to the sound of her own breathing. She discovered that she was glad to be alive, happy to have the chance to yet do something with her life. A deep, unfamiliar pleasure in her own, healthy, whole, unharmed body spread through her. For the first time in years, she felt like weeping.

She wanted to tell someone how she felt, to express a gratitude so sublime there were no words to describe it. She wished she knew how to pray.

For a timeless moment, nothing else mattered except that she lived. She forgot Joshua Carter, forgot Giffon Adams, forgot her own long-acknowledged inadequacies. She closed her eyes against a joy so potent it hurt.

"Thank you," she whispered. "Thank you."

The sound of the tow truck pulling up behind her snapped her out of her reverie. A police car could be seen coming down the road. Pulling her gloves back on, Jeri opened her pickup door and stepped out into a landscape newly appreciated. The winter scene no longer seemed bleak and forbidding; every leafless branch, every chunk of snow, was infinitely precious. An unconscious smile hovering on her lips, she went to meet the policeman.

Later that evening, Jeri walked over to Giff's office. It was past dinnertime, but he had not yet come in. She knew that he had been avoiding her, also.

He looked up when she entered, his expression unrevealing.

"I'm going out for a while, Giff," she announced evenly.

He leaned back in his chair, placed his hands behind his head. "Oh?"

"I'm just going down to Bill's, but I wanted you to know. I won't be home late."

"Fine."

"Giff...I'm sorry about all that commotion in the house this morning. It was none of my doing, you know."

"Wasn't it?"

"Giff, be fair," she pleaded, sincerely wanting to smooth things out between them.

"You going to let Carter touch you like that again?"

She stood, as tall as she could, and remained silent. She understood at last that she had a right to a private life, a life separate from Giffon Adams. She didn't know where the understanding came from, but she knew it was true.

"Well?"

"It was only a kiss, Giff. I bet you kissed lots of girls when you were Carter's age."

Giff lowered his hands to the desk in front of him. His brown eyes had taken on a slightly glassy look.

"He was just playing with you, Jeraldine. That's what made me so angry. He's had lots of pretty women. What would he want with you? You're a game to him, that's all, and he'll hurt you, bad."

"I guess I have a right to find that out for myself, don't I, Giff?" she answered, her calm voice effectively hiding the uncertainty his words aroused. "I'm not afraid of a little pain."

Giff stood abruptly. "Go, then," he said. "Go on down to Bill's. Maybe you can get another fight going." He smiled sourly at her startled look. "Did you think I wouldn't find that out, Jeraldine? I found out, several times. Quite a few people were anxious for me to know."

"Giff, I'm truly sorry. I meant to tell you myself..."

"Sure you did, Jeraldine. Sure you did. But you didn't, did you? You let me hear it from someone else."

This conversation was degenerating speedily. While her relationship with Giff had never been smooth, they had usually managed to be civil to one another. Now the wall between them confused her; she wished she knew how to tear it down.

"Well, then, you know why I have to go back there," she said softly, trying to regain her confidence. "I'll be branded a coward forever if I don't go in there and show them all how unaffected I was."

"Were you unaffected?" Giff's voice was a whipcord of intensity.

"Not really, but I can pretend real good." She smiled slightly.

Giff studied her face searchingly. She thought he seemed to relax, and he shrugged with apparent unconcern. "I'll keep a pot of tea going for you," he said, and she knew he was offering an olive branch.

Smiling more easily in her relief, she retorted, "You do that, Giff. I'm sure I'll have a story to tell when I get back." Giving him a thumbs-up sign, she turned and went out the door, happy that she had been able to hide from him the real anxiety she felt about returning to Bill's Tavern tonight. She could think of a million things she would rather do, but she knew if she were to continue to work in this community, she would have to face down whatever was waiting for her in that small, nondescript building.

Bill's Tavern was the same as always. Dark, smoke-filled, smelling of beer and whiskey, the room was already full when Jeri arrived. Stripping off her heavy coat, she took an empty seat at the bar.

The two men on either side of her silently moved away.

Susan appeared before her, dressed in her usual figure-hugging pants. Her white blouse was loose tonight and had

fine silver threads running through it. It was a pretty outfit, Jeri acknowledged ruefully. Susan obviously had no
difficulty accepting her own femininity.

"Hi, Jeri." Susan was, as usual, openly friendly.
"What'll it be, tonight?"

Jeri named a brand of beer, and a foam-topped glass appeared before her almost instantly. She wrapped a hand
around the cold glass.

She really didn't like the taste of beer. But Giff had always expected her to share a glass with him, and for his sake
she had learned to drink it. She had long ago become numb
to the fact that its actual flavor was unpleasant to her.

It was some time before Jeri realized that an unnatural
silence was settling on the room. Wondering what had
caught everyone's attention this time, she turned and faced
outward into the larger space. Still, it took her a moment to
understand that *she* was the object of observation, that
everyone's eyes in that dark tavern were regarding her
steadily and with deep hostility.

She understood immediately. Two men had fought over
her in this very place last night, and she was being given the
blame. Never mind the unfairness, the fact was that she had
never been well liked or even trusted by these hardworking
men, who saw her malelike demeanor as a threat. Now two
of their own had come to blows over her, and they were
showing their disapproval. It didn't matter that Bob
Pritchett was new in the community, or that Joshua Carter
rarely frequented the place. The regulars at Bill's Tavern
had been given a chance to show what they really thought of
Jeraldine Adams, and they were doing so with a ven-
geance.

Abruptly Jeri turned back to her beer. All her life she had
been one of the guys. It had not necessarily been her choice,
but she had fit in as best she could. She was, in fact, a bet-

ter hunter and fisherman than most of the men in this room, and she was a darned good serviceman. What right had they to turn on her now?

The silence continued, and Jeri's back stiffened. Slowly, deliberately she took a drink, then placed the glass on the counter in front of her. She noticed that Susan was hovering near, and she would have been amused at the barmaid's obviously protective stance if she wasn't so unexpectedly grateful.

Like Bob Pritchett, Susan McDougall was also new to the area. Having moved north with her husband from downstate Detroit, she had been working at the country tavern only about three months. Her husband was trying to get a new oil-exploration business going. Jeri knew from barroom gossip that money was tight for the couple, and that Michael McDougall was often out of town.

She caught the flash of Susan's wedding ring as she mixed a drink for a customer. It sat proudly on her well-manicured finger.

Jeri looked down at her own hands. She had actually taken some pains with them tonight—scrubbing them with a stiff fingernail brush and spreading lotion over them. They had soaked up the healing cream like a sponge, and she had used several applications before she had felt satisfied. Now she wondered why she had bothered. They looked just as they had before, chapped and blunt and brown where the stain couldn't be washed away.

The silence became heavy, tangible, filling the room with a malevolent anticipation.

A slow anger began to burn inside of her. She was sorry about the fight last night, but she knew that she was not the one who had encouraged it. She was sorry that these men so obviously resented her. But she had done nothing to overtly offend them. Then, out of nowhere, came a thought so unexpected that at first she hardly bothered with it. Until it returned, more strongly.

She was a failure as a man. She would like a chance at being a woman.

Another time the tiny flame of longing would have been hastily and throughly doused. Another time the sudden picture she had of herself wearing a blouse just like Susan McDougall's would have been buried before she even realized she had thought it. Perhaps it was the condemning silence that gave her the needed impetus. Or perhaps it was the fact that in the last twenty-four hours she had been kissed, twice, by the most desirable bachelor in the surrounding four counties, that had her mind spinning with suddenly possible impossibilities. Or maybe it was Giff's sullen moodiness, his willingness to think the worst of her, that had her saying, before she even knew what she was about, "Susan?"

"Do you want another one, Jeri?" Susan's tone held sympathy in it, and the contrast between that warm contralto voice and the silent hostility that surrounded Jeri was almost her undoing.

Before she could lose her nerve, she asked quickly, "Susan, what time do you get off tonight?"

Susan looked momentarily surprised, then cautiously curious. "Twenty minutes, actually. This is my early night."

"Is . . . is your husband home waiting for you?"

"No. Mike's in Wyoming. He won't be home until the weekend."

Jeri took a sip of beer and then looked Susan right in the eyes. "I was wondering if . . ." She breathed deeply. This was more difficult than she had considered. "I was wondering if you would help me, Susan. I'd like to go shopping tonight and buy a . . . buy a dress."

That was all she could get out. For the life of her, she couldn't say anymore. It was with wholehearted, if quiet, relief that she heard Susan's enthusiastic response.

"Honey, I would love to go shopping with you. But we'll have to hurry if we are able to get anywhere before the stores close. I'll just check with Harry to see if I can leave a little early." Harry, the stocky owner of Bill's Tavern, was in the back room playing pool. Often teased about the name of his establishment, he would shrug easily and reply that Bill's seemed more fitting to him, and Bill's it would stay.

While Susan was away, Jeri turned to face the men who were giving her the silent treatment. Hoping she appeared as calm as she planned, she raised her half-full mug in a silent toast.

"All right," she said, forcing light humor in her voice. "I give. I'll wear a dress and go out with Joshua Carter, if he'll still have me."

Continued silence greeted her bold announcement, and for a moment she thought she had made a terrible mistake. Then, from a far table, a cheer went up. As if a signal had been given, mugs rattled against wood, and calls of unmistakable encouragement filled the air.

"When?" someone called out demandingly.

Praying that Joshua would not let her down, she replied quickly, "I'll be back here at ten o'clock. If one of you sons-of-a-gun can track him down, it can be tonight."

The men stood, cheering and whistling and banging the table. She had won them over, all right, she told herself as she smiled stiffly. She was just beginning to wonder at the yet unknown cost of this victory when Susan appeared at her side, taking in the scene at a glance and telling her to hurry—it was almost six-thirty and they didn't have much time. With a last, deliberately casual wave to the room at large and an upward thrust of her head, Jeri pulled on her coat and followed Susan out the door.

They went in Susan's older model sedan, leaving Jeri's pickup in the parking lot at Bill's. The roads had been plowed and sanded, Susan was heavy on the pedal, and they reached the closest mall, usually a sedate thirty-minute drive, in twenty-five. As they walked with quick steps toward the main entrance of the shopping centre, Susan turned to Jeri. "Anyplace special you want to start?"

Jeri shrugged, pulling the entrance door open for them both. "Not really," she said vaguely. "I was hoping you would know where to go."

"How do you want to look? Sweet and demure? Wild and sexy? A mixture of both? Give me a hint, Jeri. And how much do you want to spend?"

Jeri was feeling more and more foolish. She didn't like being helpless, but that was what she was where clothes-shopping was concerned. Biting her lip, she looked straight into Susan McDougall's eyes. "I don't know what kind of dress I want," she said slowly. "I don't know how much I want to spend." Smiling wryly, she added quietly, "I don't own a dress, Susan. I don't know anything about buying one. Why don't you take over for me? Just don't make it too wild, or outrageously expensive, and help me be back at that bar by ten o'clock."

Susan's brown eyes widened, and she gave her tight red curls a disbelieving shake. "You're placing yourself entirely in my hands?" she asked.

"Please," Jeri said humbly, trying not to acknowledge the risk she was taking. Telling herself she could change her mind at any time, she followed Susan down the corridor full of shoppers to a small, elite store that, she quickly realized, sold not only clothing but shoes and other accessories as well. Reminding herself of a bank account that held money more than sufficient to meet her everyday needs, she allowed Susan to lead her inside.

A short while later, Jeri was wondering how anyone could possibly term shopping fun. Pulled this way and that by a determined Susan McDougall, she was subject to a series of short orders that were gradually stripping her of what little confidence she had.

"Take off your hat." Susan said, holding up a rose dress to Jeri's face. Shaking her head negatively at the style of the dress, Susan added, "Slip off your coat." A yellow garment was held against Jeri's neckline, then discarded. "Get out of those boots." Finally Susan asked the same question that Joshua had posed last night, causing Jeri to stiffen unthinkingly. "How long is your hair, anyway? Can I see?" Feeling helplessly out of control, Jeri loosed the braid, letting it hang in a dense rope down her back.

But Susan merely nodded at the thick length of it, and taking a garment from the harried salesclerk standing nearby, directed Jeri into the dressing room at the end of a long narrow corridor. "Try this one," Susan said, pushing the dress into Jeri's numb arms. "If you need any help, call me. Once you have the dress on, come on out so that we can see how we've done." Susan generously included the dark-haired clerk, whose tag announced her name was Marcia, and who had stood dumb while Susan McDougall had made decisions and barked orders with devastating speed.

By this time the whole unfamiliar shopping expedition had taken on the characteristics of a nightmare to Jeri. If she could undo the apparently uncontrollable chain of events she had started back in Bill's Tavern, she would give her whole heart to do so. But she could think of no way to turn back the clock. Like a doomed prisoner, she headed into the dressing room, the chosen garment on her arm.

Three walls of the small, brightly lit room were mirrored, and Jeri blinked at her reflection uncertainly.

Her workshirt, buttoned up to the highest button, hung loosely on her small frame. Her jeans, stained at the knees, a small tear on the right thigh, effectively covered any feminine curves she might possess. Her face was white and strained, and her pupils shone a brilliant, wary green out of overwide, stressed eyes. Her lips were held deliberately straight, a habit of expression she had formed years ago when Giff had commented on their unpleasant fullness.

Slowly, as if fighting a hypnotic trance, she began to unbutton her shirt; each time she released a button she felt she had taken a demandingly difficult step of enormous proportions. When finished at last, she let the shirt fall to the floor, kicking it aside with sudden fierce animosity. The action seemed to free her from her dreamlike state, and she reached for the zipper of her jeans, determined to finish this job as quickly as possible. When she lifted her head after stepping out of her jeans, she saw herself again in the angled mirrors.

Her underthings were white and very plain. She still wore the thick, brown men's hunting stockings she adapted in the winter for warmth. Smiling humorlessly at the incongruous picture she made, she bent to take off her socks.

Susan opened the door and peeked inside. "How are you doing, Jeri?" she asked breathlessly, only to pause in absolute, if momentary shock. "Glory be," she said. Then she smiled. "We're going to knock the breath right out of those men at Bill's Tavern," she said. "They won't know what hit them for weeks." The red-haired woman grinned impishly. "But hurry, Jeri. Hurry. Try that green dress. In the meantime, I'm going to get you some new underwear."

The dress was a rich emerald with a white Peter Pan collar. Its long, form-fitting sleeves were capped by white cuffs, and its modest length was cinched tightly at the waist by a wide, white belt. The white accents framed a bodice of delicate strands of shimmering, multicolored embroidery, sewn in an abstract design of some complexity.

Taking a deep breath, Jeri pulled on the unfamiliar garment. After laboriously fastening all the back buttons she could reach, she stared with disbelieving eyes at the reflected image that surrounded her.

Who was this person looking back at her, solemn and pale and so obviously terrified? Why, she was quite pretty, in a serious sort of way. Her face was small and delicately boned, her eyes deep pools of emerald green, her mouth straight and somber.

The dress Susan had chosen hugged Jeri's body, the smooth, luxurious material sliding over her hips and thighs, the intricately embroidered top emphasizing the curves that Joshua Carter's hands had examined only last night.

Surely this could not be herself, Adams, the furnace repairman?

Slowly she left the dressing room.

Susan looked up from where she was conversing intently with the salesclerk, her own pert beauty shining in pleasure at Jeri's transformation.

"Here." Susan thrust some packages into her hands. "That's the dress you're going to wear out of here." Susan's brisk, businesslike tone gave Jeri no chance to voice any doubts. "But first I want you to change into these. You're going to be a new woman, inside and out."

As Jeri unquestioningly turned to do as Susan ordered, Susan put a hand on her arm. "What's your shoe size, Jeri?"

Jeri looked at her blankly, then gave a short laugh. She was definitely in for the whole kettle tonight. "Five and a half," she said, before disappearing into the dressing room.

She looked at the packages Susan had given her. Silky pale green panties and bra, along with a slip of the same color and material. And a pair of sheer nylons.

Suddenly she was glad, fiercely glad. She hugged the packages to herself, and turned in three quick circles in the middle of the room. Her throat made a little gurgling noise, as if desires long repressed were trying to find utterance. She had never thought she would ever wear anything so... delicate, so beautiful. As swiftly as she could, she removed the new dress. In a matter of minutes, she was slipping it back on, luxuriating in the feel of it slithering against her new silk underwear. Examining herself in the mirrors once again, she saw that her cheeks were flushed with excitement, her eyes bright with a new and unfamiliar exhilaration.

Again Susan opened the door. "Come on," she said. "It's after eight, and we're not done yet!"

Jeri followed.

It was eight-thirty when Jeri and Susan left the mall. Jeri walked carefully in the low leather pumps Susan had insisted she buy, feeling the soft swish of the skirt of her new dress brushing her nyloned calves with each step. She clutched a bag holding her discarded work clothing in her arms.

They got into Susan's car and headed north to the tavern.

"We'll stop at my place first," Susan announced. "We have just enough time to try some makeup."

Jeri nodded, finding it easier to agree than to fight the swift, unheeding current that was carrying her to a yet unknown future.

She discovered that Susan lived with her husband in a tiny, two-bedroom house situated on one of the many small lakes that enriched this area of northern Michigan. The house was furnished in what looked like odds and ends. For a moment, a picture of Giff's home, kept neat and tidy and carefully decorated by her own hand, flashed in Jeri's mind, and with the picture came a jolt of unexpected pain. She pushed the comparison aside. Right now, odds and ends looked wonderful to her. Handing her coat to Susan, she found herself giggling.

Giggling? Only young teenage girls giggled. She clamped a hand over her mouth and followed Susan, who was walking quickly down the short hall to the back bedroom.

"Come on in," Susan called impatiently. "Ignore the mess. My beauty stuff is all here."

Following Susan's voice, reminding herself that women friends got together frequently to share feminine concerns like shopping and makeup, Jeri tried to calm her erratically beating heart. She stopped at the doorway to Susan's room.

It *was* untidy. The bed was unmade, and the thick, blue bedspread was half on the floor. The closet door hung open, and she could see both male and female clothes hanging there. A discarded slip was draped over a chair by the bed, under the slip was a man's pair of jeans. Western-style boots, obviously owned by Susan's husband, were on the floor, next to the bed. One of the dark leather boots was upright, one was lying on its side; in between was a single pink high heel. On a bedside table lay an opened package of birth control suppositories.

Suddenly Jeri felt faint, as simultaneous waves of hot and cold sensation washed through her. Making a desperate effort not to stare at the articles strewn so casually around the room, Jeri kept her eyes glued to Susan. The redhead was gathering what appeared to be an enormous amount of tubes and small containers that, Jeri knew, housed a variety of cosmetics.

Unaware of Jeri's discomfort, Susan plopped two giant handfuls of containers into Jeri's hands. Picking up a free-standing dresser mirror, Susan led the way back to the kitchen, explaining along the way, "The kitchen table is best, Jeri. The light is better, and we can spread out all we want." Relieved that she would not be compelled to spend any more time in that intimately cluttered bedroom, Jeri followed Susan down the hall once again.

Finding it difficult to regain the numbness to which she had surrendered some time earlier, Jeri seated herself on one of Susan's plain kitchen chairs. She eyed the cosmetics which she had dropped on the table with a distinct feeling of unease. "I hope you don't expect me to wear very much of this stuff," she said, almost belligerently.

Susan's generous smile appeared, mocking Jeri's obvious tension. "Just wait and see," she said with admirable confidence. "Here, open this tube of moisturizer."

Thirty minutes later Jeri could hardly believe the subtle transformation that had taken place. She had always assumed that makeup would make her look garish, but Susan, sensing her reticence, had applied the cosmetics sparingly. A creamy blusher highlighted her cheeks, bronze eyeshadow emphasized her deep green eyes, and a rose lipstick glistened on her lips. Mascara, carefully applied, coated her long, thick lashes. Her abundant brows had been gently combed with a tiny brush that had been lightly coated with hairspray.

Her hair, which she had loosed from its heavy braid at Susan's command, hung with thick waves down her back. Susan had parted it in the middle and had taken a thin ribbon of hair on each side of her head, swiftly braided each one, and pulled the two strands to a clasp on the back of Jeri's head.

"Well," Susan said, at last. "We're ready, I think."

For a minute Jeri sat quietly, unbelieving of the reflection that looked back at her from the large tabletop mirror. "Susan," she said slowly, only distantly aware of what she was asking, "why did you do this for me?"

"Because you asked me to," Susan answered simply. "Because I've been lonely and need a friend," she continued, more softly. "Because you need a friend, too."

Jeri looked abruptly down at the tabletop, neither willing to admit the truth of Susan's statement, nor deny its telling accuracy.

"I've never had a woman friend," she admitted instead.

"You do now," Susan said with gentle firmness. Then, looking at the clock, she exclaimed, "It's five to ten. We're going to be late! Come on! Come on!"

Unwilling to examine too closely feelings that were still in the fragile embryo stage, Jeri allowed herself to be led, once again, out to Susan's car. Minutes later the two women were standing outside the door to Bill's Tavern.

Jeri's hands felt damp and clammy, her stomach writhed in painful rebellion. She caught herself breathing in short gasps.

It had all been a game, so far. A silly, adolescent game. But this was no game, entering through this door to face a room full of men in her new, feminine attire. And Joshua was there already—she had seen his Jeep in the parking lot. She wondered what he was thinking; her behavior toward him had been so embarrassingly inconsistent. Her amazing temerity at summoning his presence seemed, in retrospect, arrogantly insulting, and she had the overpowering sensation that she was about to make a terrible mistake.

As panic flared, she wondered if it was possible to turn and run from the weathered door in front of her, if there was some way to back out of the suddenly terrifying agreement she had made with all those men.

Susan stood at her side, sensing her discomfort.

"I don't think I can do this . . ." Jeri began shakily.

"If not now, when?" Susan asked quietly.

Indeed. Taking a deep breath for courage, Jeri opened the door and entered Bill's Tavern, overwhelmingly glad for Susan's protective presence at her side. "Remember how nice you look," Susan whispered. "Hold your head high and look them all straight in the eye."

Quiet descended on the room as she and Susan entered. It would have actually been quite funny if she weren't so blatantly terrified. This was, after all, just Bill's Tavern. She came here three, four times a week. Her quick glance sweeping the room, she saw that there were a few other women here tonight, with their husbands or boyfriends. And there were no strangers here; she could put a name to every face.

Just last night it had been a place of comfortable gathering, of easy familiarity.

Remembering Susan's admonition, Jeri kept her head up as she slipped out of her heavy woolen greatcoat. Maintaining her falsely relaxed air with steely effort, her long, dark hair falling below her waist, she walked carefully in her unfamiliar pumps to the bar. Harry was serving.

"Adams?" Harry said, his voice a shocked squawk. "Adams, is that you?"

"The same," she admitted, and knew grateful relief that her voice gave no indication of her inner turmoil.

A low, incredulous whistle met her ears, a clear sound of enchanted masculinity that reverberated against the walls, echoed against the ceiling, and called unmistakable attention to the woman standing gracefully still at the front of the room.

"Something nonalcoholic, Harry," Jeri heard herself saying. "Please."

Susan was standing a few feet away, a watchfully supportive expression on her countenance. "You're doing fine," she said in a low voice. "Just like I said, you're giving all these jokers something to think about for a long time to come."

Bolstered by Susan's softly encouraging words, Jeri turned to face the room, the soft drink in her hand. As she did so, her dazed eyes took on a slow inventory of the stunned faces all around her. Men that she had known all her life looked at her with awe; in turn, she saw them with new sight. She saw the ones that had had too much to drink; one in particular was looking at her, squinting hard, as if she was a vision conjured up by a whiskey-soaked imagination. She saw young Billy Close, married just a couple of years, his arm slipped around a woman who was certainly not his wife. She saw tiredness and loneliness in that quiet room, and weakness and waste. And she pitied them all, and herself, who went to that country tavern night after night for the counterfeit companionship it offered.

Then Jeri saw Joshua Carter leaning against the wall that opened up to the pool room. He was staring at her with eyes that glittered savagely. Unconsciously she lifted her chin, and her eyes shifted away from him swiftly. Fighting a nearly irresistible impulse to flee, she leaned back against the bar with what she hoped was careless insouciance. Slowly she brought her glass to her lips.

She felt rather than saw Joshua deliberately push himself away from the wall where he had been leaning. She saw him reach for his sheepskin coat from a chair where it had been casually draped, she felt his leashed anger as he thrust his arms through its sleeves. She knew that his eyes had never left her face, and she felt a slow terror begin to grow as he walked in measured, emphatic steps toward her.

As he drew close, she saw that his face was a mask of grim disapproval, that a muscle was twitching wildly in one lean cheek. She turned from him abruptly; unheeding of her obvious discomfort, he took her arm in a merciless grip.

"I understand we have a date," he said, his low voice heavy with some emotion she could not recognize.

She wished herself anywhere but in this place, dressed in this fashion, being held by this man who looked as fierce as a Viking warrior. Refusing to let him see the panic in her eyes, she kept her gaze fixed on the shelves of bottles opposite the bar. "I..." she stammered slightly, "I...you don't have to, Carter. I didn't mean to force you, or anything."

But he was already pulling her away from the bar, his arm around her waist, his body shielding hers from the stares of all the gawkers at Bill's Tavern. "We're getting out of this dive," he said, his voice low and fierce. "Now." Unerringly he reached for her coat and shrugged her into it with rough haste. Meeting Susan's concerned eyes over Jeri's head, Joshua's expression softened momentarily. ".When is Mike going to be home?" he asked with seeming irrelevance.

"Saturday," Susan told him.

"Tell him I suggested the four of us get together for dinner," Joshua said softly.

Susan smiled, but her gaze was on Jeri's misery-filled eyes. "I'm sure we'd like that," she said.

Nodding, Joshua half pulled, half carried Jeri toward the outer door. Just before opening it, he thrust Jeri behind him and turned to face the darkened, smoke-filled room.

"Remember this," he said, his even tone hiding none of his arrogant possessiveness. "Jeraldine Adams is mine. Don't even think of trespassing. And any one of you who treats her with less than the utmost respect will answer to me."

Suddenly everyone seemed to have someplace else to look. Conversations resumed, drinks were remembered, a pool game continued.

Turning swiftly, ignoring the smattering of drunken applause that erupted somewhere behind him, Joshua put an arm around Jeri's shoulders and walked her quickly out the door.

Chapter Five

The door to the tavern banged shut behind them. Her mind mercifully blank, Jeri pulled away from Joshua's imprisoning arm and began to stride toward her own pickup. Stepping forward carelessly in her desperate, instinctive haste to rid herself of Joshua's suffocating presence, her newly heeled foot hit a patch of ice. She would have fallen if Joshua had not caught her arms and held her upright.

"Where do you think you're going?" Joshua asked, his tone frighteningly quiet in the clear cold air of the parking lot.

"Back to Giff's house," she said, icily defiant.

"The hell you are. You made a date with me, and now you're damn well going to keep it."

She rounded on him suddenly, saying with a kind of tortured vehemence, "I was making a point, Carter. Nothing else. It's late. Nothing will be open anymore. There's no place to go. I want to go back to Giff's."

The tavern's pole light made Joshua appear darker, more shadowed, as his eyes raked her scornfully. "You were making a *point,* Adams?" he demanded coldly. "You know, it wasn't very convenient for me to come over here tonight. In fact, it was damned inconvenient." He gave a short, barking laugh. "And now you tell me that all of this was so you could make some ridiculous point, that you don't mean to honor your very publicly spoken pledge at all?"

Biting her lip in frustration as she silently acknowledged her own foolishness, she turned away from him quickly. Hopelessly she cursed the insane urge that had started her on this futile scheme earlier in the evening. Staring at the side of her blue pickup, she said through gritted teeth, "All right, Carter. Where do you want to go?"

"We'll decide that after you're in my Jeep," Joshua said tersely. "But I know a few places."

Again taking her arm in a gesture so proprietary it was all Jeri could do not to jerk away, he walked with her to his vehicle. When she would have opened the door, he pulled her back sharply.

"No," he said with a hard edge to his voice. "This is a real date, Adams. I'll be treating you just like I would any other woman with whom I might desire to spend some time. Which means I open the doors, among other things. Understood?"

Throwing him a confused glance, she stood silent while he pulled the passenger door of his Jeep open. It was a high step, and she felt his hand on her elbow, assisting her into her seat. Carefully arranging her coat so it would lie free of the door, Joshua smiled at her crookedly. "Relax, Jeraldine," he said. "You might even find what's left of the night enjoyable."

"Quit...calling...me...*Jeraldine*," she demanded through closed teeth. Before Joshua, only Giff had ever called her by the lengthened form of her name. And she was never quite sure whether Joshua's use of it was some hidden form of intentional mockery.

But to her surprise, he looked at her with real consternation before saying with quiet courtesy. "Of course, if that is what you prefer."

Puzzled by this unexpected display of friendliness, she shifted swiftly so that she was staring straight ahead at the Jeep's dashboard. Seeing her tightly closed expression, Joshua's mouth twitched as if with some private amusement, and he shut her door with gentle force.

He took her to an out-of-the-way Italian restaurant in the lakeside town of Charlevoix. Surprisingly unusual for mid-January in northern Michigan, the restaurant stayed open until midnight. After they were shown to the corner table Joshua had requested, she felt his hands on her shoulders, helping her out of her coat. His touch took her by surprise, and she closed her eyes momentarily, instinctively swaying towards him. His hands stilled; she felt their heavy weight linger on her shoulders. Stiffening slightly, she shrugged away from him, trying to recapture the anger that had been boiling all too close to the surface.

She heard him sigh, but she refused to glance at him when he pulled out her chair so that she could be seated. Joshua stood for a moment at her back, and she felt his fingers lightly caressing her neck. "I like your dress...Jeri," he said, before he moved to take his own chair at her right.

The lighting in the room was dim, and the single candle burning at their table created a softly intimate glow. While the restaurant was not empty, there were no other diners near them, and she knew Joshua had chosen this secluded spot deliberately.

She was surprised when Joshua inquired as to her preference when ordering, for she had thought that he had intended to play the petty dictator for the duration of the evening. When the food was brought, steaming hot and wonderfully aromatic, she discovered she was quite hungry. She had not, she remembered, had any dinner and was grateful that her appetite gave her something to do as the silence between them had begun to stretch uncomfortably.

Joshua ate leisurely, seemingly unaware of her increasing tension. From time to time she glanced at him uneasily, noting with growing discomfort that his eyes rarely left her face. She was reminded of his unwavering regard the previous night in Giff's kitchen.

When she could bear it no longer, she asked brittlely, "Why are you staring at me?"

He brought his hand up to trail one finger slowly down the length of her cheek. "I stare because you are so beautiful," he said softly.

Jerking away from his touch as if stung, she felt bitterly betrayed by her own pervasive sense of exposed vulnerability. The feeling was intolerable. Hoping her desperate self-consciousness did not show, she reached for her wine with fingers that, incredibly, were not shaking.

"Still scared, aren't you, Adams?"

"I don't know what you're talking about, Carter," she retorted evenly, hiding the resentment that flared at his reference to the other time when she had fought, terrified, in his arms.

"Yes, you do," he said, his blue eyes holding hers with inexorable intensity. "You're often frightened. It shows in the shadows of your eyes when you think no one is looking. It shows in the way you hold your body, proud and distant, like a frozen snow queen, too cold to touch."

She looked away from him swiftly, finding no words to deny his cruel description. There was a burning behind her lids, and she felt shame that she was allowing him to see her pain.

"Do I really look like that?" she could not keep from whispering, her hands clenched in tight fists under the table.

"Sometimes." His voice had gentled, as if he knew the anguish he had just caused her. Once again his hand grasped her face, and he forced her head around until she was compelled to meet his gaze. The angry arrogance in his eyes was gone, replaced instead by a knowing intelligence, a sympathetic understanding that caused her to close her eyes tightly. But it was too late—a single tear made its lonely way down the contours of her face.

"But not tonight," Joshua said with almost coaxing softness. "Tonight, my dear, you are unmasked, and you are all that is brave and warm and innocent. Even if you are still frightened."

"You are mocking me now," Jeri said quietly, looking at the candle burning steadily in the center of the table.

"No," he said. "I do not mock you, Jeri. I merely say what I see, what everyone at Bill's Tavern saw. You shamed them, Jeri. When you walked into that room, all soft and feminine and beautiful, there was not a person there who was not aware of your courage. There was not a person that could not know he was seeing an act of bravery so profound that he was unworthy to witness it. All these years they thought they knew you, only to discover a stranger behind your walls, a woman of guileless beauty, whose innocence and loveliness were still undefiled. And you were so unaware of your own attraction, of your own power. You shamed them all."

"They are my friends," Jeri said. "I had no intention of making them feel that way."

His fingers were wiping away the moisture on her cheek. She took a shuddering breath, blinking fiercely, as another tear crept down her face.

"Which person there is your friend?" Joshua asked. "Slow-Mo?" he used the nickname of one of Harry's regulars, "who sits and drinks every night until Harry won't sell him any more? How about Tim Fee? His Friday paycheck is gone by Wednesday, and his wife has to leave her children so she can work to earn enough to feed the family. Or is Billy your friend? He changes sleeping partners like other men change shirts."

Taken aback by Joshua's observations, Jeri remembered her own quick, uncommon insight as she had faced the familiar group at the tavern tonight. Yet, unreasoningly, she thought she ought to refute his damning accusations.

"I...*you* go there."

"Jeri, I've been in that bar exactly five times in the last three years, and every time I've had only one reason for doing so."

She could not prevent her eyes, glassy with the effort of holding back tears, from flying up to meet his questioningly. His smile was a grim expression of self-mockery. "To see you, Jeri. Every time to see you."

That information was both too precious and too painful to contemplate. She pushed it away temporarily, along with the joy that had surged quick and strong at his words. "Susan..." She tried to turn from him, not wanting him to see her eyes, but his hand kept her face toward him. "Susan is my friend." Her voice had taken on a chokingly desperate defiance.

But Joshua merely nodded. "And I have it on the best authority that she's quitting next week."

Dread swept through her at the thought of losing her new friend so quickly. "How do *you* know she's quitting?" she snapped.

"Mike McDougall and I go way back. In fact, he moved up here on my recommendation. He's wanted Susan out of there ever since she started, but she felt she had to find a new job first. Now she's got one, and she's leaving Bill's."

"What ... what will she be doing?"

"What she has trained for. She's a color analyst, and she's been hired by one of the department stores in Traverse City as a consultant."

No wonder she had moved so quickly tonight. Susan really had known what she was doing.

The conversation about Susan had taken her mind off herself. Tears no longer hovered so perilously near.

Joshua's hand was still on her cheek; in an unconscious gesture of uncharacteristic trust, she raised her hand and caught his in her own, then lowered them both to the table.

"I'm glad for her," she said truthfully.

Joshua was watching her intently. "But *you've* quit tonight, Jeri. You've drunk your last beer at Bill's. You won't go back there again."

She bristled automatically at his autocratic words. "Who are you to tell me what I can and can't do?" She tried to pull her hand away from his, but his tightened grip would not allow her freedom.

"You are my exclusive territory, Jeri," Joshua said, his words so soft that she had to strain to hear them. "And I am yours."

"Joshua ..." she began, then stopped abruptly. She had no knowledge of flirtation, and she wondered dazedly if this conversation were normal among men and women. And if it were, how did one react?

Again she tried to pull away from his grasp, but for all her effort, he only glanced down at their clasped hands. For a moment he was impassive. Then, holding her wrist against the pristine white tablecloth, he spread her fingers out for his slow perusal.

She waited for him to make some new comment on their work-roughened state. When he did not, she found herself saying defensively, "There is nothing wrong with my hands, Carter. They're honest. They've worked hard. And they know their stuff."

Surprisingly, Joshua agreed. "That's right," he said, massaging her skin lightly. "But when you are mine, your hands will not look like this, all rough and bruised and unprotected."

The tears she had thought conquered were again dangerously close. Holding her breath with the effort of forcing them back, she looked swiftly away. "Are soft hands a prerequisite for womanhood?" she asked in a tone of repressed despair. "If so, I fear never to reach that exalted position."

"Not soft hands," Joshua said, his clear blue eyes offering wisdom beyond her comprehension. "Just healed ones."

It was as if he were speaking a language foreign to her, and she had been left without any one to interpret.

"Every cut, every bruise, every wound can be healed, Jeri," he continued. "The healing will not make you soft. It will make you strong."

"My hands are strong already, and you speak in riddles. I am quite finished. I would like to go now."

Still he did not loose his hold on her. No longer looking at her face, he traced the line of her fingers one by one, as if he was memorizing their texture in the dim light of the candle.

"Did you hear me? I said I was ready to go."

"Tonight that is not your decision to make," he reminded her simply. "And we have not yet had dessert."

"I don't want any," she said, sounding childishly sullen.

He smiled at her slightly. "But I do," he said, and once again the conversation had shifted its emphasis. Jeri felt an invisible pull so strong she almost cried out. Joshua was wrong; she was not so innocent. Sometime in the last thirty-six hours she had gained enough knowledge to recognize immediately the potent intensity of strong sexual desire. It was like the call of a child to its mother, like the need to breathe when air has been withheld too long. Her own breathing became more shallow; her eyes glazed slightly. Instinctively her lips parted.

"No," Joshua said, shaking his head in rueful understanding, although she could see that his eyes had darkened in quick response to her uncalculated hunger. "Not tonight. Perhaps not ever, Jeri Adams."

The stroking against her fingertips was a contradiction of his words, so that the feel of his fingers brushing rhythmically against hers became almost unbearable. Involuntarily she closed her hand in a fist so tight her knuckles shone white in the candlelight. She felt herself trembling slightly.

"Have I no will of my own?" she asked, quietly desolate. "What have you done to me?"

His laughter, though light, held an undertone of bitterness. "What have *you* done to me?" he asked. "You are an exquisite enchantress tonight, so full of beauty and so incredibly desirable. I fear I may never recover."

"Please," she said. "I don't want you to talk like that. I don't understand it, and your words make me feel alien, as if... as if I am a stranger in my own body." She looked at him, her wide green eyes hiding none of her confused arousal. She heard her blood pounding heavily in her ears. "Please, stop," she whispered.

His eyes acknowledged her anguish, and his lips quirked upward briefly. "All right, then," he said. "Tell me how you got the knowledge and expertise to do what you have done with Giffon's house."

She was startled and showed it. "Giff's house?" she queried blankly.

"Yes." He was watching her carefully. "The decorating, the stenciling."

"Did you . . . did you like it after all?"

"I thought it was exceptionally wonderful, Jeri."

Pleased beyond reason, released from the strange tension that had caused her chest to constrict and her thoughts to jumble maddeningly, she smiled at him tentatively. And though his eyes narrowed at her slight show of unguarded friendliness, his carefully controlled expression did not change.

"Well," she spoke seriously, hardly knowing what she was saying in her shy pleasure, "Giff always just let me do whatever I wanted." She clasped her hands together and fell silent, remembering the times when Giff had come home to find a new piece of furniture already in place, or a freshly painted wall, or a new item of decoration. He would smile that smile that told her he found her infinitely amusing, and she would wilt like a storm-beaten wildflower.

Now, with slowly dawning horror, she remembered that Giff had promised to wait up for her, had promised to have the teapot simmering. How could she have so stupidly forgotten? Abruptly standing, she said in a panicked voice, "I really have to go, Joshua. It's late, and—"

Joshua had risen with her. "What's wrong, Jeri? Will Giff be pacing the floor, wondering about my intentions?"

Ignoring the frustrated anger evident in his tone, she asked desperately, "What time *is* it?"

"Almost one," Joshua said, maddeningly calm.

"Oh, no," she said. "I told him..." She looked at Joshua beseechingly. "Please take me back," she begged.

Joshua's eyes never left hers, so that she could not help but see the hard mockery that colored his bleak expression. Yet something in her desperate demeanor had him agreeing, albeit acidly, "All right, I'll take you back." He paused, then said with telling emphasis, "Much against my better judgment, I'll deliver you back into Giffon's... loving...hands."

About a mile from the tavern where Jeri's pickup was still parked, Joshua pulled off into a roadside rest area. He didn't turn off the Jeep's engine, neither did he turn on the interior light.

Acutely aware of every minute that made her later still, Jeri, tense and resentful of the extra stop, waited for him to speak. Obviously, however, Joshua shared none of her sense of fierce urgency, for he sat almost relaxed for a moment, looking out into the starlit winter night.

"I would like you to decorate my house," Joshua said at last, turning toward her slowly.

"Your house?" she queried uncomprehendingly.

"Yes. I'm afraid it's quite huge, and the only room with any furniture in it is my bedroom. Will you furnish it for me?"

Even while her brain registered the enormity of the compliment she had just received, she was saying with frank disbelief, "Come on, Carter, I'm a furnace serviceman, not an interior decorator."

"I would pay you, then. Whatever interior decorators get paid. That should make your status official enough."

"No," she replied quickly. "It's out of the question. I do not have enough time."

He reached out in the warm darkness of the Jeep to run his fingers across her lips.

"You could make time, Jeri. For me."

Only her swiftly indrawn breath told him of her reaction to his touch, but it was enough. Half turning in his seat, using his hand to guide her face, he brushed his lips lightly across her own.

"Will you look at it and then decide?"

"I . . . I don't know Joshua. I . . ."

His fingers were massaging her temple now. It was just a gentle touch, a friendly touch; yet it held her spellbound in its power.

"Say yes, Jeri," he ordered softly, his face just inches from her own.

She closed her eyes to keep from seeing his shadowy form. She thought of Giff waiting for her. After the scene in his kitchen this morning he was likely to be furious with her lack of consideration tonight, and the reason for it. Still, the urgency that had been drawing her back to Giff's side seemed vaguely diminished. She felt again the slight movement of her new dress against her body. With compelling clarity, she understood that the choice she had to make involved much more than Joshua's request.

"Jeri?" Joshua said.

"All right," she said slowly. "I'll look at your house. But no promises beyond that, Joshua."

She thought he relaxed slightly. His hand dropped to clasp one of hers where it rested on her lap. "Saturday," he said. "I'll pick you up at nine, and we can spend the day together. We won't have to meet Mike and Susan until around seven."

She had forgotten Joshua's carelessly worded commitment to Susan earlier in the evening. She had not agreed to the dinner—she had not even been asked. Yet she could summon no resentment at the thought.

She had wanted to find out what it was to be a woman. Who better to teach her than Joshua Carter? She tossed her head back in an unconscious gesture of defiance. "Saturday will be fine," she said.

"Good."

When they arrived at the tavern's parking lot, Joshua turned to her and said, "I'll follow you home." Waving her protests aside with what she was learning was his customary determined arrogance, he continued, "Wait for me when you get there, and I'll see you to the door."

The drive that had taken so long last night in the blizzard took just a short time tonight, and it was only minutes before she was pulling down Giff's long driveway. Joshua, true to his word, pulled up right behind her. Her lips curving in an involuntary half smile, she waited by the side of her pickup for him to join her.

Putting an arm around her shoulders, he walked her slowly to the door. As they reached the lit porch, he pulled her around to him with deliberate slowness. Content to follow his direction for what surely would be their last few minutes together, it took Jeri a moment to comprehend that Joshua was staring, frowning, at the door. The knob was turning, and in her dreamlike state, she automatically reached out to touch it.

But before her hand reached the brass fixture, the door was thrown open from the inside. Light poured out onto the shoveled porch, and Jeri raised suddenly frightened eyes to see Giff standing in the doorway. Her hand went out to the older man, but there were no easy words of explanation on her lips. She had the suddenly strange sensation that she was somewhere else, that the body standing there on that porch belonged to someone else. She struggled visibly to regain the identity she had somehow left behind her hours ago.

She felt Joshua shift beside her, felt his body suddenly relaxing as he pulled her against him more intimately. Giff's eyes, hidden in shadow, absorbed in silence Joshua's tall figure standing with deliberately indolent arrogance.

Then, ignoring Joshua Carter completely, Giff said, "You do know what time it is, Jeraldine?"

Her initial relief at his calm, even tone was swiftly buried as Joshua's voice sounded from behind her. "Why, it's one-thirty," he said in mock surprise, making a show of examining his watch even as he tightened the arm that lay possessively about her shoulders.

Giff stiffened. With the light at his back, the older man's jeans and deep blue shirt appeared almost black. The illusion added a sinister quality to the stiff angle of his neck, the rigid tautness of his body, and Jeri stared at him, as if Giff were a stranger that she was meeting for the first time. Yet his voice was familiar, revealing nothing except disappointment when he stated with heavy irony, "Jeraldine has never allowed anyone to speak for her before."

Joshua shrugged insolently, dismissing Giffon Adams's criticism with a single lift of the brow. "It is cold out here," he said softly, his eyes locking with those of the older man. "We would like to come inside."

Giffon Adams settled more firmly into his position in the center of the doorway. "Jeraldine may enter at any time, of course," he said smoothly. "But, as I'm sure you understand, it's late, Carter."

Turning from Joshua, Giff was reaching for Jeri before she had a chance to realize his intent of forcibly pulling her inside the house. "I'm positive you will have a good reason as to why you are so late, Jeraldine, and why you didn't call," Giff was saying silkily, his arm outstretched toward her demandingly. But Joshua was swinging her gently but quickly to one side, so that Giff's hand brushed against

Joshua's sheepskin coat impotently. Seemingly unaware of Carter's maneuver, Giff continued, "Or perhaps I need seek no further explanation than that found on my doorstep." His reference to Joshua Carter was an open insult.

"You bet she has a good reason, Giffon," Joshua said, his low voice like a sudden sharp whip in the night air. "The best in fact." Joshua paused briefly, making sure he had Giff's full attention. "I've been courting her," the younger man continued, "and she liked it, too."

There was a knowing smile on Giff's lips as he lifted his hands, palms outward, in a gesture of peace. "Of course she would," Giff said, almost placatingly. "Of course she would. After all, what does Jeraldine know of a man like you? What chance has she got against your very practiced charm? What words did you use with her tonight? Whatever you said, I bet you didn't tell her how many women you have had in the last year, did you? Did you happen to mention how many times you've scored recently, Carter?"

Giff's voice was so calmly friendly, so reasonably persuasive, that it took a moment for Jeri to assimilate the dark intent of his terrible words. "No!" she blurted unthinkingly. "It's not true!"

Yet, even as she cried out the hot denial, she knew a seed of doubt had been placed with cruel accuracy in her heart. What did Joshua want with someone like her? He could have anyone he wanted, just like Giff said. Earlier this evening Giff had told her, had tried to warn her, that she would be nothing more than a game to Joshua Carter. What other possible reason could he have for seeking her out? She, Jeraldine Adams, who hardly knew how to buy a dress, let alone wear one, was surely not an acceptable companion to someone like Joshua. None of it made any sense to her.

Then Joshua's voice sounded over her bowed head. "The world is quick to judge by its own standards, Giffon. Believe what you will, it's nothing to me. But don't tell Jeri your lies."

Relief burned through her, like a flame heating an icicle so frozen it cracked in the melting. With rare intuition, she knew that whatever else Joshua Carter was, he was no liar. When he told her she was beautiful, it was because he believed it. When he talked of healing, he believed that, too.

She raised her head slowly, only just now realizing how she had sought to bury it in Joshua's chest. Pulling away from his sheltering strength, she turned until she was facing Giff. "This is ridiculous," she said quietly, trying to hide the searing pain his anger caused. "I'm not a teenager whose chastity needs your constant protection, Giff." She paused, letting the words sink in, watching Giff as his eyes narrowed at her. She knew that Joshua would see nothing in Giff's face, but she saw things. She knew that her words had infuriated him, but worse than that, she knew that Giff also was afraid. For the first time she realized her own importance, that Giff was terrified of losing her. Instinctively aware that the danger of confrontation was past, she reached out to touch his arm. "I'm going inside now," she said gently. "Joshua is coming with me. I'm going to warm up some of that tea you were saving for me. Perhaps you would like to join us for a cup?"

She turned to Joshua and nodded at him. Watching her enigmatically, the blond man moved to follow her into the house. Giff, stunned at the way Jeri had suddenly taken control, moved back silently. She smiled at him reassuringly, trying hard not to see the hatred flare hard and bright in his eyes.

As if in slow motion, Jeri removed her coat and hung it on its hook in the mudroom. More conscious than ever of her feminine clothing, she could sense Giff's eyes on her in shocked disbelief. Moving to make the tea, she forced herself not to turn around, or to acknowledge in any other way the impact her new clothing and hairstyle might have on Giffon Adams. She heard the sounds of Joshua also removing his coat, and in spite of herself, she was glad that he was still there.

She had certainly given no thought to the consequences of her individual actions tonight. She had simply reacted, and now the chips were falling uncontrolled in a myriad of different directions. If she had stopped to think about Giff, she would never have gone on that crazy shopping spree with Susan. If she had considered her words, she would never have summoned Joshua, would never have had dinner with him. Yet she could not find it in herself to be sorry. She felt strangely illuminated, as if the changes she had effected and the decisions she had made caused her to see with a brighter, clearer vision.

When the tea was poured in the cups, she finally allowed herself to turn around. Joshua was standing with one hip against the table. Giff was standing in the doorway, much as he had done this morning. Only now he looked older, more tired. It was as if the sight of her in her emerald dress and her hair down had defeated any words he might have said. Sensing that his ancient discomfort with her femaleness was causing him to feel a stranger in his own house, she looked him straight in the eyes and said, "I've a cup of tea for you, too, Giff." Her voice was all that was soothing. *Forgive me,* it said.

But if she had hopes for a true reconciliation, they were quick to be dashed.

"Did you dress like this for *him?*" Giff asked harshly, jerking his head in Joshua's direction.

She chose to say the truth. "Yes."

"In spite of what I told you this afternoon."

"Yes."

"I never knew you valued my opinion so little," Giff's voice was condemningly harsh.

"Giff...I...it actually feels good, Giff, to be wearing a dress. Other women wear them, after all."

Giff snorted.

For the first time since he had entered the kitchen, Joshua spoke. His voice was neither low nor conciliatory. "You might as well know, Giffon, that Jeri will be seeing me on a regular basis. Now, I believe that she'd old enough to know her own mind, without any help from you. But just in case there's any misunderstanding, you should be aware that she'll be out with me several times a week. You need to know that she'll be wearing dresses, using makeup, and leaving her hair down, just like she did tonight. If you have a problem with that, old man, speak now. I won't have her condemned for behaving naturally, or for her association with me. There are plenty of places for Jeri to live, beside here."

"Is this true?" she heard Giff demand of her. "Are you going to do as he says?"

She realized with a sense of dismay that both men were looking at her intently. She felt Giff's unreasoning, jealous anger, and she felt her newfound confidence begin to slip. Then his face changed, his expression became sad and grieved. Guilt pressed down on her like a heavy, suffocating cloak.

"I..." she began uncertainly.

Joshua's hand reached out to squeeze hers, hard. She heard her knuckles crack as the pressure grew intense. Frightened, she looked up at Joshua; he was watching her with relentless impassivity.

She glanced away from him swiftly, her eye pausing as she noticed the counter clock, an old antique in the shape of a small church. It read two o'clock. She felt strange, her spirit somehow separated from her body, and knew a weariness that had nothing to do with the late hour.

Before tonight she had made few actual choices. She wished now it were not so. She wished she had some experience that told her she was capable of deciding wisely.

Finally she whispered, "Yes...I'm going out with Joshua Carter." She could not look at Giff.

For a moment only silence met her announcement. Then Giff said in a voice that sounded strangled with the effort of speaking, "So be it, Jeraldine. I wash my hands of it. When he's used you and ruined you and thrown you away, don't come running to me for comfort. You won't get any from me. You've made your own choice this night, and a bad bit of work it will turn out to be, but so be it."

For a moment she felt a pain inside of herself that she could not bear. It was like a rupturing of bonds that, though unseen, were strong with the force of years. Just when she thought she could stand it no longer, she looked into Joshua's eyes. Admiration was written there, mixed with concern and a deeper emotion that she could not name.

A whisper of a sigh escaped her lips, and as if permission had been given, she began to experience a new and unfamiliar feeling of peace. As last night's storm had left behind an earth newly white and clean and unmarked, so her soul seemed to be resting, newly purified.

Joshua's hand loosened against hers. "Go to bed, Giffon," he ordered softly. "We don't need your sick opinions anymore. I want some time with my girl."

Giff glared at him, hesitating, from the doorway. "You've washed your hands," Joshua said to him. "Now get out of here, or I take her with me, now."

For a moment the two men stared at each other, but it was Joshua who seemed the most menacing. Finally Giff's right hand made a fist, and in an angry, impotent motion he pounded it into the doorjamb. Then, turning abruptly, he stalked through the living room into his part of the house. The sound of his door slamming shut echoed in Jeri's mind for a long time to come.

Get 4 Books FREE
SEE BACK OF CARD FOR DETAILS

FREE MYSTERY GIFT

We will be happy to send you a free bonus gift along with your free books! To request it, please check here and mail this reply card promptly!

Thank you!

BUSINESS REPLY CARD

FIRST CLASS MAIL   PERMIT NO. 717   BUFFALO, NY

POSTAGE WILL BE PAID BY ADDRESSEE

SILHOUETTE READER SERVICE
3010 WALDEN AVE
P O BOX 1867
BUFFALO NY 14240-9952

NO POSTAGE
NECESSARY
IF MAILED
IN THE
UNITED STATES

Chapter Six

On Wednesday Jeri resumed her full work schedule by using her pickup as a makeshift service vehicle. She made three service calls and two emergency repairs—not a heavy day by midwinter standards. She returned to Giff's house in early evening, only to discover that he was not there.

She sighed heavily. Her continuing conflict with Giff was like a festering blister on her mind. If she refused to think about it, she could almost believe it was a figment of her imagination. But it rubbed the borders of her consciousness at odd moments, making her feel raw and uncertain.

Giff had certainly made no attempt today to heal the widening rift between them. He had been up and in the office before she had even arisen, even though she had not been late. When she had called the office to offer to carry him a cup of coffee from the house, he had refused curtly. And later he had handed her the list of today's jobs with a sharp gesture of open animosity, his eyes meeting hers for the first time that day, speaking wordlessly of betrayal and abiding anger.

Tight-lipped, she had taken the list and strode quickly out of his office. She had not seen him since. And now it was dinnertime and he was not here.

But Giff was not the only person occupying her thoughts today. Visions of Joshua Carter had flitted in and out of her conscious mind with predictable regularity.

For years she had been certain that Carter despised her, and the awareness of his scorn had hurt more than she had ever admitted. Now she hardly knew what to make of their new relationship.

She thought of his kisses, of his fingers brushing across her lips, and felt her face flush and her heart begin to pound in erratic anticipation. She remembered the way he had touched her as she stood with him in the guest bedroom just two nights ago, and the memory was so suddenly sweet that she caught herself swaying, as if straining toward his embrace. Yet she knew with absolute certainty that it was neither his touch nor his kisses that had her caught in a fragile web of terrified expectancy.

Some other man might have touched her and caused no new awakening. Another might have kissed her and found no quickening response. No, she was not so stupid as to try to fool herself that it was merely Joshua Carter's hands and lips that had set her trembling a hundred times today.

It was his eyes, blue as the winter sky, that seduced with secret understanding. It was his voice, low as the lakeside breeze, that enticed with the promise of hidden treasures of knowledge.

He had not stayed long after Giff had walked out last night. Just long enough to drink half a cup of tea and to kiss her lightly good-night. Before he left, he had once again mentioned Saturday's date, as if he wanted to be certain it was fixed firmly in her mind.

She laughed soundlessly. As if she ever could forget. Like a giddy teenager, she had worried all day about what she would wear. Her closet was barren of feminine apparel, and she could hardly wear the emerald dress for a date that started at nine in the morning. She looked at the clock. It was only a little after six. With almost frenzied swiftness, she stripped out of her coat and headed back to her private bath to take a shower. With a little luck she could be dressed again in fifteen minutes. Driven by the ungovernable elation singing suddenly through her veins, she decided to try a little shopping on her own tonight. After all, she told herself defiantly, Giff's absence was giving her silent permission.

Joshua arrived at nine o'clock sharp on Saturday morning. She was alone in the house; Giff had disappeared sullenly when she had told him she was going to spend the day with Joshua Carter. Breathlessly she opened the door to Joshua, saying with what she hoped was calm normality, "Good morning."

"And good morning to you." He smiled at her, his eyes flicking over her briefly, before returning for a more intimate perusal. She was wearing a pair of purple designer slacks, topped with a lighter violet sweater. Across the front of the sweater was a snowscape of white spangles that curved around her figure. Her hair was braided but unbound. It hung in its familiar thick rope down her back. Later, when they went out for dinner, she would loosen it.

That her outfit met with Joshua's approval was apparent by the pleasure in his gaze. Greatly relieved, she motioned for him to enter. "I'm just about ready," she said.

She had him sit in the living room while she went to get a small overnight bag. Not that she was planning on staying overnight, she told herself wryly. Knowing that she would not be returning to change for dinner and wishing to be prepared for any contingency, she had packed a skirt exactly the same shade as her slacks, some nylons, a pair of new black heels, and a few articles of makeup she had daringly purchased on her solo shopping spree Wednesday night. Even her coat was new. With its wide shoulders and slender waist, held tight by a thick belt, and the double row of silver buttons down its black front, the coat had been irresistible; she had paid for it without blinking an eye at its high price.

While Joshua waited, she penned a note to Giff. *I'm sorry you weren't here to say goodbye,* she wrote. *I'll be back sometime tonight.* Then, hesitating, she finally decided on a plain *Jeraldine.*

A late model red Ferrari was parked in the driveway, and Jeri, upon seeing it, turned to Joshua in stunned surprise. "This is not your Jeep," she said incredulously.

He smiled at her crookedly. "No, but it is mine."

With her knowledge of things masculine, Jeri easily figured the Ferrari's approximate cost in her head. Shaking her head in disbelief, she turned to him as he opened the door of the sports vehicle for her. "I never knew you owned anything like this," she said in open admiration.

"I haven't kept it hidden," he replied almost teasingly. "I just don't usually drive it to job sites, or in snowstorms."

She waited for him to get in his own seat before saying curiously, "You didn't use it Tuesday night, either, and it was not storming then."

He turned the key in the ignition, and the car roared into action. They had driven out the driveway and onto the road before he replied briefly, "No, I didn't use it then."

"Why not?" she prodded.

He shrugged. "I had not done the asking for that date, Jeri. I knew you were using me, and I was willing, but I was determined not to provide a damned carriage like an obedient pet prince."

Quickly she looked away to the rolling winter landscape that seemed to be flying past her window. "You are hardly anybody's idea of a pet prince," she said with stiff resentment, recalling with vivid memory how scared she had been on Tuesday night. "But I'll remember about your royal male pain-in-the-ass ego in the future."

His lips quirked. "Sure, babe," he said. "You remember all you can about me... in the future."

She bit her lip in frustration at her own stupidity. Of course there was no guarantee there was going to be any future between them, and even if there was, her last asinine comment was certainly not what an experienced woman would say to any man in whom she was interested. She stared stolidly ahead.

Joshua made a sudden choking sound that sounded suspiciously like buried laughter, but when she looked at him with swiftly flaring anger, his face was an innocent mask of bland pleasantness. Burying her hands in the pockets of her new coat, Jeri stared out the window as if the familiar passing landmarks were fascinating archaeological discoveries. She did not once glance Joshua's way again until he had pulled up in the driveway of his home.

While driving to and from jobs, Jeri had often peered at what she could see of Joshua Carter's home through the dense stand of trees that lined his property. And she knew from her previously unwilling, if also unconditional, respect for Carter's work, that he knew how to put together a beautiful building. Still, nothing had prepared her for her first sight of Joshua Carter's house, as he followed the winding driveway around the trees and up a gentle slope that led to his home.

The first word she thought was *grace*. The second was *honesty*. The third, *beauty*.

Built utilizing a series of cantilevers, the building seemed at once suspended by the most fragile connections, and yet firmly grounded in the natural terrain surrounding it. Sided with redwood, much of the house was encircled by a large deck. The roofline sloped in direct imitation of the slant of the earth. An abundant and unusual placement of windows made her immediately curious to see the inside of this unbelievable abode.

Using an automatic door opener, Joshua pulled the sports coupe next to the Jeep in an attached garage that continued the architectural line of his home.

"Well, we're here," he said impassively. "You will want to see the inside, of course."

"Of course," she said faintly, filled with the bitter knowledge that there was no way she had the skill to decorate a structure such as this one. She knew it, and she knew Joshua Carter must know it.

Still, she offered no resistance when he led her through the adjoining door into the interior of his home.

They entered into a hallway that led to a spacious, modern kitchen on the right, and a coatroom and half bath on the left. Allowing Joshua to hang up her coat, she followed him to the kitchen, her mind absorbing its plentiful cupboards, the large island work area, the windows that bowed outward slightly in what was obviously a breakfast nook. Along another wall, large sliding doors led out to the deck, which, she saw, had been thoroughly cleaned of snow.

Next to the kitchen was a formal dining room, again with wide, expansive windows that overlooked the deck and the large meadow beyond. The floors were all beautifully finished hardwood.

The line of the floor and ceiling led naturally into a massive room, where one wall was made up entirely of natural fieldstone, which surrounded a fireplace of enormous proportions. The opposite wall had the same floor to ceiling windows that had been in the kitchen and lined the dining room. But here the wooden flooring was laid to form a rich mosaic of circular design, starting at the middle of the room and radiating outward. Jeri realized as she studied the floor that the great room itself was in the center of the house, that all rooms flowed from it in a contrapuntal design of exquisite harmony. And then she thought, this house is a song. It sings of hope and faith and love.

She was silent as Joshua led her through the rest of the structure. She discovered that in addition to the rooms she had already seen, its three levels contained four bedrooms—each with its own private bath. Other rooms included an office, a family room, and even a full basement. And, as Joshua had said, only his bedroom was furnished.

Joshua had used only tans and browns in his room, and the resulting monochromatic scheme was as peaceful as it was masculine. A king-sized water bed dominated the room; she could not help but wonder at his need for so large a bed. Jeri noted without surprise that this room also had a wall of windows, and that a door led out to the deck, much as it had in the kitchen. There was also a fireplace here, with two wing chairs placed on either side of it. A small table was placed near the windows. Papers and books were littered across it, as if Joshua had only just now risen from one of the side chairs, leaving his work open and unfinished in anticipation of his early return. An electric coffeepot sat on his dresser. Two closed doors led, she guessed, to a private bath and to a closet.

She felt like an intruder. Her walls seemed to be caving in on her, squeezing her, leaving her no room to breathe or to think. She felt her control slipping. "Very nice," she murmured, and turned with barely concealed haste to leave Joshua's room. His arm slipped through hers companionably as they made their meandering way back to the center of the house.

It was all light and space, even with the rooms naked and empty, and Jeri could have cried for the beauty of it. At some point in their walk through the house she had come to the unbelieving conclusion that Joshua Carter was dead serious about her decorating his home, and she knew with futile desperation she would have to disabuse him of the notion quickly. Yet awe and a kind of yearning hunger kept her silent until they ended their tour where it had begun, in the kitchen. Jeri walked to the sliding doors, rubbing her arms as if she felt a sudden chill.

"How much land do you own?" she asked flatly, looking out at the expanse of snow-covered ground.

"Forty acres," Joshua replied. "Enough to plant a garden, enough for children to get lost in."

She turned to face him, her expression set and pale in her determination. "Builders must make a lot more money than I knew, Carter," she said. "This place must have cost a fortune."

He shrugged. "Most of the work I did myself. It took me a long time." He was watching her intently, and with a sudden jerking motion she brought her hands up in a gesture of defeat.

"It's beautiful," she said, almost angrily. "It's more beautiful than any house I have ever been in." She swung around so that she was once again facing the outdoors. "It's obvious you built it for a woman," she said more quietly, trying to hide the sense of desolation that she felt. "You must have loved her very much."

She heard Joshua sliding his back down a wall so that he was sitting on the golden ceramic tile floor. Turning abruptly to face him, she saw that his hands were supported by his upraised jean-clad knees, and that he was watching her unwaveringly. "Come here," he said softly.

For a moment she simply stared at him. He was so beautiful, so ruggedly handsome, just like this house. The sweater he was wearing was sunlit yellow; the light streaming in from the windows caught its color and blended it with the warm tones of the floor, causing Joshua Carter to appear as if he were surrounded by a pool of light.

His voice grew a little harder, dispelling the illusion. "Come," he said again.

She walked slowly to where he was sitting, allowing him to grasp her hand and tug her down next to him on the floor. His arm came around her shoulders, forcing her close to him. Her head fell forward until it was lying on his chest.

His hand began a slow rubbing motion up and down her arm. "I was engaged once," he said. "I thought you knew that."

She had not, and she shook her head to tell him so, even as she was hit with the painful realization that he was confirming the truth of her statement, that he had built the house for someone else.

"Over five years ago," he continued. "Her name was Helen, and we had known each other all our lives. I was going to bring her up here to live, but our engagement ended, and she never came." He made a light fist and brushed her chin gently. "She has never seen this house," he said.

"But you built it for her," she insisted.

"I built it for what I thought our future might be," he said. "But she would never have been happy here. After our engagement dissolved, I realized that this place was my vision, that there was almost nothing of Helen in it." He brought both his arms around her body, holding her close. "You have no reason to be jealous of Helen."

She stiffened. "I am not jealous," she denied.

He lifted her chin. "Good," he said. "That's very good, since there's no cause. Still, when I kiss you in just a moment, I want you to know there are no shadows of other relationships lurking around. There's just you and me, babe."

She looked at him questioningly but had little time to wonder at his words, as he pulled her head up just enough so that he could bend his to kiss her.

This kiss was different from all that had gone before. She was beginning to realize that kisses came in a seemingly endless variety, and this one was friendship, acceptance, and subdued desire. Yet there was comfort also, and she found herself leaning into him easily to accept the kiss. The cold tile floor was beneath her, and the hard wall was at her back. Joshua's hand was hard, too, as it held her head firmly, forbidding escape. In contrast his mouth seemed soft, almost tentative. Warm and nonthreatening.

Then, sensing her acquiescence, he deepened the kiss. Her hand came up to rest upon his chest. He twisted his body so that she was practically lying across him. She felt one of his hands move to her nape while the other supported them both from the floor at her side.

Time ceased to exist. Winter morning sunlight bounced off the blanket of snow outside and flooded the room with its promise of warmth. The house seemed like an oasis of heat in the frigid north, and the hottest, brightest part of it was in the kitchen where Joshua and Jeri sat exploring the feel of each other's body.

It was Joshua who eventually pulled away. His lips left Jeri's, a slight groan escaped his throat, and he pulled her so that her head was against his sweater, tight. He leaned back against the wall, one leg still propped up in its angled position, the other straight out in front of him. His breathing had quickened, and she knew an unfamiliar and completely feminine satisfaction that he was so obviously struggling to regain control. As if unaware of his own movement, he raised his hand to stroke her face. Her braid fell over her shoulder and onto the floor; absently he began to toy with one long strand that had come loose from its constricting bands.

She felt incredibly warm and safe and more alive than she could ever remember. She liked kissing Joshua and knew joy in the realization that she was not a sexless male copy, after all. Her strong physical response to this man who now held her in his arms validated her existence in a way never before experienced, and a tuneless melody seemed to be accompanying the rhythmic beating of her heart. *Woman, woman, woman,* it sang.

"Do you understand what is happening between us, Jeri?" Joshua asked huskily.

"No," she answered truthfully, "but I like it when you kiss me."

Laughter rumbled deep in his throat; she could feel his chest shake against her cheek. "That's a start, babe," he said, almost tenderly. "But you're such an innocent, you probably don't realize that I would like to do a lot more than kiss you."

She resented his continued assumption of her childlike purity; she was, after all, a daughter of her time. "You would like to have sex with me," she said, utterly calm. "I am ready, I think."

His arms tightened around her almost convulsively, and she waited with expectant longing for him to kiss her again. When he kissed her, life seemed so easy. There were no choices to make, no feelings to hide, no inadequacies of which to be ashamed. There were only sensations and responses so intense that her normal barriers were, for the moment, rendered useless. It was exhilarating, like the first time she had ridden a bicycle or driven a car. Yes, she liked kissing a lot.

It took her a long moment to realize that he was, after all, not going to resume their intimate embrace. In fact, once she had emerged from her cloud of pleasure, she had the definite impression that even though he was holding her tighter than ever, he had withdrawn from her completely.

"You certainly get right to the point," he said at last, and she could have cried at the coldness in his tone. "Tell me, Adams, what do you think 'having sex' means?"

His icy rejection had her shrugging in instant insolent response. "I know how people procreate," she said. "I've had the appropriate classes in school. And the guys in the bar talk about it often enough."

"I just bet they do. In full graphic detail. And speaking of procreation, are you by any chance using any birth control, Jeri?"

She was silent for a long time. Of course she was not using anything. Unbidden, the picture of Susan's open box of suppositories flashed in her mind. She remembered the unmade bed, the tangle of male-female clothes strewn about her new friend's bedroom. Closing her eyes against the image, she replied quietly, "No." Then, because she thought that she was being punished for a yet unrealized sin, she added with some bitterness, "You know I have not done this with anyone else but you, Carter. You will be my first."

He gave a short bark of laughter, but his tension had eased somewhat, and he resumed his slow stroking of her arm. "Maybe I will, Jeri. And maybe I won't. But in any event, it will not be today."

His hand felt so good against her body, it was all she could do to keep from purring like a cat and cuddling even more intimately against him. "But I want you to," she said, as if stating the fact proclaimed the eventuality. "I have always wanted to know what it was like. I won't ask you to marry me, or anything. Promise."

He rose slightly, thrusting her away from him in sudden anger, so that she fell to her knees a foot or so away. Catching her balance, she looked at him warily, made aware by his forbidding expression that she had said something dreadfully wrong.

"You make this sound like some dumb high school laboratory experiment," he told her jeeringly. "And we're both some sophisticated sort of guinea pigs."

Disappointment coursed through her. Maybe it was dumb, but just for a moment she had felt real joy in the knowledge that soon she would be initiated into the timeless mating dance in which men and women had participated since the beginning. And she had wanted it so badly. She, Jeraldine Adams, who until this last week had only a future of lonely spinsterhood ahead of her, had just come heartbreakingly close to having a memory of passion to hug near in all the cold, winter nights of her life. Fear that she was about to lose the only chance she might ever have of experiencing what it was like to be a woman gave her the strength to face him with fresh defiance. Unheeding of his newly aroused temper, she began to speak to him with hurried desperation.

"Come on, Carter," she taunted lightly, striving for the right tone of amused reproach. "Even I know it's not fair to light the oven if you don't plan on having dinner."

He rose to his feet in one quick, uncoiling motion. "Human intimacy is much more than a mechanical act called 'having sex,' Adams," he said, looking down to where she remained kneeling at his feet. "If you don't know that, you don't know anything."

Reaching down to grasp her hand, he pulled her roughly to her feet. "And quit looking like such a damned supplicant," he said. "I'm no randy bull to take you here on the kitchen floor."

"You're not a pet prince!" she cried out in frustrated rage, her hands clenching at her sides. "You're not a randy bull! Oh, you're full of what you're not, Joshua Carter. Well, maybe you could tell me just what you are, and why I'm here, and what this is all about."

But the shutters were back on his eyes, and the expressionlessness was on his face, and he merely replied quietly, "That's something you'll have to work out for yourself, Jeri. In the meantime, maybe we could discuss your ideas for decorating my house."

She left him then, walking blindly in an agony of humiliation and despair. Her still aroused body mocked her efforts at reassembling her battered emotions. He was impossible to understand, she told herself with furious self-disgust. After all, it was *he* who had kissed her. It was he who had seduced with his hands and his eyes and his body. He had no right to throw her willingness back in her face as if she had offered him something tainted.

She found herself in the great room, leaning against the stone fireplace, her hands wrapped around her waist. She decided she hated this house. She hated its perfection, its openness, its honesty. Which was a good thing, because

Joshua Carter could not pay her enough to even consider helping him furnish his house, now. There was no way she would spend any more time with him than necessary. She wanted to go back to Giff's.

Stonily she gazed at the open space in front of her. In spite of her hard thoughts, almost without meaning to, she began to reexamine the empty spaces of the large room.

As she did so, she knew with inner surety that she had the capabilities of filling this room, of furnishing this magnificent building. She could suddenly see it all: hard against soft, circular against straight, old against new. Oh, she could do it all right, she told herself with smug self-righteousness. But she wouldn't, not for Joshua Carter, who was obviously playing some malicious game with her, just as Giff had said.

His hand on her shoulder made her jump. "I'm sorry," he said simply. "You have every right to hate me right now."

"I do," she said, refusing to look at him. "I hate you, Carter."

"But I couldn't do it," he continued. "I couldn't take what you offered, much as I was tempted. You're too new, Jeri. New and fresh and unknowing. You didn't really understand what you were saying."

"I did," she said. "I'm twenty-four years old, Joshua. I understand perfectly everything I said. You just didn't want me, that's all."

"I want you all right, Jeri. I want to love you." His hand was massaging her shoulder lightly.

She jerked away from him and strode across the room. "You just want to make a fool out of me," she accused him, her green eyes glowing bright in her fury. "And you succeeded, didn't you? You had me begging, didn't you? Isn't that enough? You can brag about that easy enough down at

Bill's Tavern. Jeraldine Adams begging you to love her. Ha!''

"What I *want* is to love you," he repeated, a glint of challenge in his electric blue eyes.

"Huh," she said, her voice raw. "You had your chance. It will be a cold day in hell before you get another one."

"I want to *love* you."

She hated him. She hated that low voice, which stripped her of her pretenses and left her feeling naked and empty and yearning. It was all she could do to keep from putting her hands over her ears in a childish gesture of rejection. "Take me back to Giff's," she demanded roughly.

"I want to love *you,* Jeri. But not in haste, not in lust, not without commitments." He had walked to where she was staring sightlessly out the window. His arm was around her shoulders before she could move away, and it was no longer a gentle touch that held her. "I'm not taking you back," he said. "I'm sorry I didn't understand your need, and I'm sorry that I hurt you, but I'm not taking you back."

"I...you..." she began, then found she could not speak.

"Why won't you let yourself cry?" he asked. "Why do you fight it like this, holding in your grief until I ache just watching you?"

"It's you that makes me cry," she spat at him angrily, trying to pull away. "Leave me alone, and you will be spared the no-doubt nauseating sight."

Putting both his arms around her, Joshua pulled her to his chest. "Not me," he said. "It's not me that makes you cry, Adams. It's hearing the truth that does it. Maybe you should ask yourself why the truth makes you sad, Jeri."

"What truth?" she asked rebelliously into his sweater front, trying to deny the pleasure she found there.

"Truth that says you are beautiful and desirable and a pleasure for me to be with. Truth that says I liked holding you and kissing you, and I'm sorry that I caused you pain."

She did not know what to say, so she said nothing. She was conscious of a great welling grief inside her, a feeling of mourning, as if someone had died. She was terribly afraid that any second she was going to lose control, and then she was going to make a fool of herself, indeed.

Something of her tension must have communicated itself to him, however, because he ceased speaking, and instead stood silently holding her against him, leaning his head down to hers. She had the crazy notion that he was trying to absorb her sorrow, that he was sharing her pain.

And she no longer wanted to leave. She wanted to stay here forever, encircled by his arms, leaning on his strength. The anger and hatred drained out of her, and she closed her eyes, wrapped her arms around Joshua's waist, and accepted the gift he was offering.

When the danger of tears was past, when the feeling of peace between them was so intense she was sure she could taste it, he turned her so that she was facing outward into the great room. His arms remained around her, under her breasts, and she leaned back against him with new ease.

"Well," he said. "Tell me what you see here in my room."

"I . . . I'm not sure I can," she began with shy hesitancy. Now that her anger was gone, she was uncertain of her original impressions. And she had never before explained to anyone how the shapes of things formed themselves in her mind. She remembered a high school paper in which she had attempted to put her sense of shape and style and beauty into words. The paper had been returned to her with spelling and punctuation errors heavily marked in red. It was the last time she had tried to put in words what she was able to see with her heart.

She felt Joshua's hands touching her rib cage, she felt his chest rising and falling against her back. "What do you see?" he asked again.

Her hands clasped together nervously. "I can't really believe you want me to do this, Joshua," she said.

"Tell me," he said.

Taking a deep breath, she began, "I see shapes and spaces, that's all. It's so hard to explain. I see the room like a...like a canvas. And ideas of what to place where come and go with some..." She searched for the right word to convey what she was feeling. "With some degree of fluidity. This is a very new and modern house, yet I see many old and well-used pieces here. What I see is...contrast, and in the contrast I feel...harmony. I see curve against straight, soft against hard, and always honesty and light."

She shrugged helplessly. "That probably makes no sense at all."

"Try again," he urged. "Be more specific."

She walked away from him to lay her hand upon the fireplace mantel. "For instance, here," she said, gaining confidence. "I see a collection of old hand-held farm tools. Their shapes, whether curved or straight, are usually smooth and dark, providing contrast against the light fieldstone you have placed here. And the tools were created for the power they gave the farmer to control his environment, to defy the rock."

She paused, searching Joshua's face for his response.

"Go on," he said softly, his eyes on her face.

She walked to the windows. "Here, I would place a table. Not necessarily an antique, but I would look for a table where the shape and line of the wood was repeated in the table itself. I know of a man on the other side of the Peninsula who makes the kind of table that I'm speaking of. With the spectacular view you have outside, placing such a table right inside the window makes the transition more gradual, from the natural lines of the outdoors to the more controlled ones of civilized living. You could eat here occasionally, or work here, or just sit and read, and feel at home with both your environments."

In her growing enthusiasm she threw him a totally unguarded look and caught an expression of genuine wonder in his eyes. "I knew you were the right person for this job," he said.

She had forgotten her control; she felt her face go hot with unexpected pleasure. It was sheer luxury to speak so freely and to be heard, to be understood. For a moment she stood, looking at Joshua, and grinned like an idiot.

Then slowly her pleasure faded. "It is a lovely home," she said, almost wistfully. "And I would have liked to work with you on it. But I really can't commit the time. I'm usually working six or seven days a week and will be doing so at least until late spring. Then Giff will have me in the office, helping him catch up on paperwork." She turned from him, unwilling to let him see the extent of her disappointment.

"You're a free agent," Joshua said quietly. "Tell Giffon Adams to hire someone else to handle the overload."

She drew in a sudden sharp breath. So simple a solution, so difficult a task. "It's just not possible..." she began.

"Why not, Jeri?" he asked, then said softly, "Make the time, for me."

His words repeated those spoken in his Jeep last Tuesday night. But she wondered if he knew just what he was requesting. He was asking her to choose. He was asking her to defy Giff for him. Yet she had already done so, just by being with him today, by dressing as she was, by kissing him as she had. In fact, ever since she had entered the bar last Monday night, she had been defying Giff. She wondered if Joshua knew how that defiance had been tearing her apart. At night she had been having strange nightmares, and during the day she had been tempted to do anything, make any promises, to effect a reconciliation between herself and the man who had raised her.

Joshua Carter walked across the empty room and took her suddenly lifeless hand in his warm grasp. "How about one day a week?" he asked. "Couldn't Giffon do without you one day a week?"

She looked at him, and even though his touch was gentle and his gaze was warm and persuasive, she saw stark fury in the depths of his clear blue eyes.

"You really hate him, don't you?" she whispered.

"I hate what he has done to you, Jeri," he said gravely. "But what I feel is not the issue here." Then he repeated his earlier question, "Will you commit to me and my house one day a week, Adams?"

Fear welled in her. To say yes meant, I will spend time in your home, and it will be only you and me here. To say yes meant, I will make changes in my life for you. To say yes meant, I will defy Giff for you, I will bear his rage for you, I will feel guilt for you.

"I will pay you," Joshua said, as if offering further incentive.

"No," she said sharply. "I would not want to be paid. I have always sold my time for money. I do not need any more."

"You would do it for pleasure, then," Joshua said, and she knew from the satisfaction evident in his tone that she had given herself away.

"All right," she agreed, suddenly harsh. "One day a week, although at that rate this entire project will take about five years."

"Good," he said, smiling slightly. "Five years of seeing you regularly is a nice commitment, for starters."

For a moment he stood holding her, and she was comforted by his undemanding embrace. Yet it was not long before she felt again the hunger he had roused. She instinctively moved against him, letting him feel her need, then stilled in true panic as she remembered his cruel rejection in the kitchen. She felt him stiffen against her, felt his hands grip her more tightly. His breathing became more shallow, and when she dared to look at him, his eyes were dark orbs of desire.

But when he spoke, it was of a different kind of hunger. "It's after twelve," he said, his voice ragged as he struggled for self-control. "Let's go find someplace to eat. And after that, I have a little surprise in store."

"Surprise?" she queried, looking at him.

"And how long has it been since you've been roller-skating, Miss Adams?" he asked, forcing a light, teasing note into his voice.

Roller-skating. Not since she was a child, light-years ago.

"Roller-skating?" she asked, looking at him doubtfully.

"Sure," he answered easily. "We'll pretend that we're just kids, without any worries at all, for the duration of the afternoon. Just two young kids, roller-skating for the heck of it. Deal?"

And suddenly she wanted to do exactly as he said. To be young again, to be unaware of the appetites of her body, of the deficiencies of her character.

Suddenly innocence seemed to be the most desirable state of all.

Chapter Seven

Jeri was ten years old again, and she was racing, the feeling of speed and motion like wildfire flowing through her veins. She was one with the upbeat music, moving her feet in time to the steady rhythm playing loudly from the speakers that hung from the ceiling. She could hear the sounds of others all around her, yet she felt alone, isolated in the intensity of her pleasure, aware only of her feet skimming the ground, of her body leaning forward slightly into the wind her own movement created, of her arms balancing her small frame with familiar skill. For the duration of the race, her isolation, her pain, her guilt, could be briefly—and oh so wonderfully—ignored. For the usually solemn preadolescent girl, this concentration on the movement of her strong, young body gave her a rare taste of what it was to be free.

And then the music stopped. Coming out of her trance, Jeri looked around to see other skaters slowing, leaving the floor, and heard with disbelief her name being announced as the winner of the women's speed race. Joshua was standing beyond the curved barrier that surrounded the smooth wooden floor, looking at her with open approval, a huge smile splitting his face.

"Congratulations, Jeri!" he yelled.

She waved at him, grinning foolishly, before skating to the MC's box to collect her prize: a ticket for a free skate on another day. Feeling absurdly proud, she left the floor to join Joshua in the spectators' area, the free ticket gripped tightly in her hand.

He had turned so that he was leaning with his back against the short wall, both elbows resting on the flat top. Braking too late, she rolled into his chest; one of his arms came up to catch her against him. For a moment they were both thrown off balance as their roller skates tangled and their hands caught against each other and the wall. By the time they had stabilized, her arm had found its way around his waist; his was around her shoulders. "Surprised you, didn't I?" she said, waving her prize ticket in front of his eyes.

"Constantly," he replied, then bent his head to brush her lips in a light kiss. "Having fun?" he asked.

Her only response was a quick smile and a flash of her eyes before she turned away from him, her emerald gaze searching the crowd of Saturday afternoon patrons for the face of a young girl she had noticed earlier. The child was sitting on a carpeted bench near the rental desk, removing her skates. She looked to be about eight years old, although her slight frame made it difficult to judge with any degree of accuracy. The girl's white-blond hair was pulled back in a ponytail. Her jeans, into which her shirt was neatly tucked, were just a bit too short. Jeri observed the girl, red-faced from exertion, speaking with quick animation to a tired but pleased-looking young woman who was sitting next to her. Losing no time, Jeri pulled away from Joshua and hurried over to the pair.

"Excuse me," she said, kneeling in front of the girl. "I couldn't help overhearing earlier that this was your first time roller-skating."

The girl nodded shyly, glancing up at the woman who sat at her side.

"Did you enjoy yourself?" Jeri asked.

"Yes." The girl nodded with youthful enthusiasm. "And I only fell down twice."

"Why, that's great," Jeri smiled. "Perhaps the next time you come you won't fall at all."

The woman sitting beside the child stiffened, an involuntary frown causing her face to look suddenly pinched and old. The girl glanced at her uncertainly. "May we come again, Mother? Please?"

"Perhaps." The answer seemed deliberately evasive to Jeri. She knew that even an afternoon at a roller rink could be considered a luxury for a young struggling family.

Glancing at the mother reassuringly, Jeri said quickly, "I won this ticket just now, but I probably won't be coming back here for a long time. Maybe you would like to have it." She pressed her prize ticket into the young girl's hand.

The child's face lit up, and she turned to her mother in quick appeal. "May I, Mother? May I please?"

The smile on the young mother's face was somewhat forced, but she answered readily, "Of course, Anna. And now, what do you say?"

Jeri accepted the girl's thanks, made aware by the determined set of the mother's shoulders that she had shamed them unthinkingly. Turning to the woman impulsively, she said with quiet sincerity, "I'm sorry if I'm out of turn, here. It's just that she reminded me of myself, years ago. She was certainly having a wonderful time out there."

The young mother's smile became more natural. "She *was* having a good time. I do thank you." Her tired brown eyes followed her daughter as she took her skates to the rental counter. "She makes it all worthwhile, you know?" And on that somewhat all-encompassing statement, the woman rose to place her arm around the girl's shoulders in a quick tight hug. Smiling at Jeri one more time, mother and daughter turned to leave.

Jeri watched them go, aware of a swelling in her throat that had not been there earlier. She knew a swift, sharp ache of loneliness. She had never known her own mother, and she never thought to be one, either. Suddenly aware that the pair were taking their time gathering their coats, she raced with quick resolve to the entryway of the rink.

"Please," she said to the man who stood there, counting tickets. "When the little girl with the ponytail and the red coat comes through here with her mother, please give them a month's supply of free passes. Tell them it's a prize or something. I'll pay, just as soon as they leave."

The man looked at her assessingly. Then, nodding slightly, he turned from her, ostensibly to get something from under the counter. She moved away, inordinately pleased, knowing that he would do as she asked. Skating back to the floor, she found Joshua moving easily at her side.

Uncomfortably aware that he had witnessed her spontaneous act of generosity and thinking that he might find her foolish, she smiled at him in some embarrassment. But his eyes were dark and warm as he inclined his fair head toward her. "They're announcing a doubles skate," he said. "Be my partner?"

If it had not taken her long to remember her old skill using the heavy skates, she had also been quick to recognize a kindred spirit in Joshua Carter. He, too, was fast on the floor, and he moved with athletic grace that outshone any other patron there. Now, with one of his arms in front of her and one at her back, she placed her hands in his and leaned into him, asking laughingly, "Are you a secret skate professional? You do this very well, you know."

His arms helped her turn as they rounded a corner. "Actually, I haven't done this in years. But when I was in high school a group of us used to do this every week, and if I may modestly say so, we got to be pretty good."

"Was Helen in your group?"

The words were out before she even realized she had thought them, and she immediately wished them unsaid. But Joshua answered without hesitation, seeming neither amused nor surprised at her question. "Yes. But she had another boyfriend then, and I another girl."

After that she didn't ask any more questions. Of course Joshua had had plenty of girlfriends. Of course his ex-fiancée would have gone with more than one boy. It was she who was the freakish exception. She had no previous relationships with pursuing men, either young or old, to guide her through the unaccustomed delight she felt every time Joshua's eyes rested on her. She had no practice at all in dealing with the strange emotions that filled her heart and made her light-headed every time Joshua's peculiar, crooked smile was aimed her way. She felt like she was on the edge of some steep and cruelly jagged precipice, and she feared it would only be a short time before she fell and was impaled, lifeless and bloody, on some yet unseen stony outbreak, miles below.

Yes, it was almost painfully pleasurable, this feeling of being sought after, wanted. Yet it was a very fine feeling indeed, to feel Joshua's arms around her, to constantly be touched by his eyes and hands and body. She wanted to laugh out loud with the sheer joy of it. She would not look to tomorrow, or beg trouble from the future. And if trouble came, well, she remembered her words to Giff, so bravely spoken. *I can stand a little pain.*

She could too, she told herself staunchly. And she was willing. She would risk the unknown future in order to enjoy this miraculous present. For today, Joshua Carter wanted her, Jeraldine Adams. She would deny him nothing, nothing at all.

Jeri was still floating on her cloud of blind pleasure when she walked with Joshua into the restaurant that night. Susan and her husband had already been seated, and Mike Mc-Dougall stood as she and Joshua approached. She was not surprised when Mike greeted Joshua with the familiar ease of long friendship, his eyes resting on Jeri in curious appraisal as he waited for Joshua to make the introductions.

She had time to realize that Mike McDougall was an extremely tall man, dwarfing both Susan and herself, and standing a good six inches taller than Joshua. Broad of shoulder and strong of limb, Mike exuded a raw male essence that momentarily rattled Jeri. Unaccustomed as she still was to being given any special notice from the opposite sex, the admiration that gleamed from Mike's expressive brown eyes had her cheeks turning pink and her hands twisting into each other nervously. She found herself amazed that Susan had ever felt comfortable enough with this giant of a man to date him, let alone enter into the marriage contract.

Mike was hardly conventionally handsome. His cheeks were broad and strongly boned, his lips wide and full. His shaggy eyebrows almost met in the middle of his forehead. His hair, thick and dark, was cut in short, even layers. He had a beard that, while neatly trimmed, added to his slightly piratical appearance. The pale blue dress shirt he wore atop a pair of obviously new jeans did little to tame what Jeri was sure was his naturally rugged appearance. Jeri thought of the jeans she had seen in Susan's bedroom, beneath the casually draped slip, and she shifted her eyes away in sudden hot discomfort.

Joshua's hand was at her back as he said, "Jeri, this small man in front of you is a friend of mine of many years, Mike McDougall. Mike, meet Jeraldine...*Jeri*...Adams."

Mike grinned. "I see Joshua has stolen the plumb from all the locals. I'm sure glad to meet you, Jeri."

Her immediate reaction was astonishment at Mike's smooth compliment. Then relief swept through her as she realized his sincerity. Joshua's hand was on her shoulder, squeezing her with quick comfort, before he pulled out her chair so she could be seated. She wondered if Joshua realized how much of a stranger she felt in her new clothes, how she was struggling to hide her fear behind her brave new identity. She saw Joshua's eyes meet those of his friend in confident acceptance of Mike's quick assessment and realized with a sense of shock that Joshua was actually proud to have her by his side.

And then she thought, perhaps all the old tales are true. Perhaps he is a prince, and I...I am his princess. And this is fairyland.

He certainly looked regally golden in the restaurant's light. She could not help but notice how Joshua's fair, symmetrical features carried with them a male beauty unequaled in the room. And his casual clothes—a loose tan cotton shirt paired with the cotton twill pants that rode comfortably on his muscular hips and thighs—could not have looked better if they had been tailored for a king.

Everything is so easy for him, she thought. He has no walls; he takes for granted his own appeal. He is so sure of himself and the loyalty of his friends.

Susan, on her right, reached over to squeeze her hand. "You look beautiful, honey," she said.

Jeri swung her gaze around to meet the dancing eyes of her new friend. Susan's short red hair was swept high and up off her forehead, giving her a look of polished sophistication. She was wearing a deep brown velvet jacket over an apricot blouse, and her makeup was flawlessly applied.

"Do I really look all right?" Jeri asked shamelessly. "Oh, Susan, how can you say so?"

Susan looked at her critically. The makeup Jeri had purchased had not seemed quite right when she had tried it at Joshua's house, and she had finally washed her face clean and settled for black mascara and a colorless lip gloss. She had changed to the straight, hip-hugging skirt she had packed and loosed her hair. After several futile attempts at more complex styles, she had finally parted it down the middle in the simple fashion of a school girl.

"I say so because it's true," Susan said firmly.

Jeri relaxed. It was far better than her most elaborate childhood daydream, sitting next to Joshua Carter, sharing his friends and his confidence and his laughter, catching him looking at her at odd moments with a curious light of possession in his blue eyes.

None of them knows, she thought. None of them realizes that for me this occasion is as rare a gift as a rose in winter. I wish I could press the petals of this experience in the book of my remembrances. I must pay close attention to everything, memorize everything, so that I can hoard this memory exactly as it happened, that its warmth may thaw forever the frozen places of my heart.

Conversation dipped and swelled around her, and she knew she participated in it, that she made appropriate responses, laughed at appropriate times, listened with a sense of power and intensity heretofore unexperienced. She knew that her eyes were probably shining, revealing for everyone to see her newly found enchantment.

By the time their waiter cleared their dessert dishes, Joshua's hand seemed to have found a permanent resting place on her knee, his fingers intertwined gently with her own. "How long are you home for, this time?" he was asking Mike.

"Three days," Mike answered with a shrug, his brown eyes flicking with unguarded tenderness over his wife. "Three short days."

Jeri saw Susan's eyes cloud with quick tears as the redhead looked swiftly away, angrily bringing a hand up to wipe her cheek. Mike's face creased in concern, and he caught Susan's hand in one of his larger ones as she lowered it to the table. "Ah, honey," he said.

Susan glared at her husband, half in anger, half in longing. "It just doesn't seem fair," she said.

"I know, honey," Mike said, shifting uncomfortably. "I know it's hard on you." He looked as if he would have said more but stood instead, bringing Susan with him. "Let's dance," he said to his wife.

Jeri watched in silence as Mike and Susan walked to the dance floor. Mike folded his wife into his arms, and they were soon dancing, cheek to cheek, thigh to thigh, heart to heart. Susan's arms reached up to encircle Mike's neck, and the tall man bent to her, his hands moving with the rhythm of the music to caress her body. Joshua smiled crookedly. "I don't think they will want to wait too long before heading home," he said.

"No," she agreed, understanding.

"I'm glad you have gotten to know Susan a little better," Joshua said. "She has been terribly lonely since moving here."

I did it because I need a friend, and so do you. For the first time, she realized the depth of sincerity underlying Susan's words. It had not occurred to her that Susan might truly need a friend just as badly as she did.

"She wants to have a baby," Josha said. "But she's afraid to get pregnant without any emotional support nearby."

A baby. It would take courage for Mike and Susan to start a family, considering their long separations. Oil-field marriages were notoriously high divorce risks. "I wonder if they can do it," she said, speaking her thoughts aloud. "I wonder if their marriage will survive the strain."

Joshua immediately understood what she was saying. "Susan and Mike are neither one quitters. I think they will last. Just be her friend, Jeri. It will help her more than you know."

"I have little experience in being anyone's friend," Jeri admitted softly. "But I would like to try to be Susan's."

"Good," Joshua said, a glint of satisfied approval in his eyes. "Now, how about following the example of our dinner partners? May I have this dance, Miss Adams?"

She froze. "Uh . . . Joshua . . ." she began.

He was already standing, his hand held out to hers.

"Josua . . . I can't . . . that is, I don't . . ."

His eyes crinkled in quick understanding. "It's easy," he said. "I'll teach you."

With obvious reluctance, she rose slowly and allowed him to lead her to the dance floor. "Here," he said. "Put your hand here, on my shoulder." He folded her other arm so that their two hands were clasped between them. "Slow dancing is really simple," he said. "Just follow my lead."

"What happens when the music goes fast?" she whispered fiercely.

"One step at a time, babe," he murmured. "One step at a time."

What was it about this man, that every time he held her she felt so cherished and comforted? What was it that caused his arms to give her the illusion of coming home, a world-weary traveler safe at last? Why was it that she felt her will begin to slowly seep out of her, and yet she knew no fear or resentment? Joshua's body became more important to her than her own. She could feel his heart beat against her palm that was held tightly against his body; her own heart seemed to pump only in response. She could feel his chest lift and fall as he breathed and knew her own breath was keeping time with his. As if in a haze, she felt the beginning of his arousal; he communicated it to her through a touch that became deliberately less possessive, from the angle of his head as he intentionally turned it away from her, from the almost imperceptible tensing of his muscles as he began to impose upon himself restraint.

She, on the other hand, seemed to have lost completely her own control. Joshua's feelings became her feelings, his thoughts her thoughts, his eyes her eyes.

And she, at last, began to see herself as beautiful. She saw as if in a dream how her long, shining hair swayed and shimmered in an unwitting dance of seduction; she felt the intensity of Joshua's desire to bury himself in its thick strands. A vision fell on her, full-blown, of herself lying naked, her hair a mattress of streaming silk beneath her, and she knew Joshua's hunger had created the picture in her mind. She saw, with a gathering sense of awe, that her body was infinitely lovely and almost tormentingly desirable to Joshua.

Yet she also saw his pain as he withheld himself from her. She sensed his struggle as he refused to take that which she would have willingly given him. She sensed his will and knew it had been forged in a furnace hotter than any she had ever known.

Why? she cried to him in silent supplication. *Why do you refuse yourself? Why do you refuse me?*

His hand was at her waist, touching her lightly, communicating no fierce desire. She found that although her head had fallen forward until it rested against his shoulder, he had not pressed it closer. She wondered if she had imagined it all, if her own need was filling her with hallucinations. Yet when she raised her head to look at his face, she knew that it had been no imagining. For she saw pain there, and struggle, and strength.

"Why?" she whispered.

He shook his head, refusing to meet her questioning eyes. "Dance is over, I think," he said. "Susan and Mike have left. It's time for us to go, too."

She discovered she was trembling.

Obediently she followed him off the dance floor. He threw some money on the table and helped her into her coat. Taking her arm and looping it through his, he walked her out to his car. She barely noticed the frigid cold of the outdoors blasting at her as a heat such as she had never known burned feverishly through her veins.

Joshua gunned the engine; the Ferrari roared through the night. Inside its small enclosure, neither Joshua nor Jeri spoke.

He parked on the driveway outside his home, not bothering to raise the garage door. Leaving the engine running, he turned to her and said, "I'll get your case. You wait here." And she understood that he was giving them no time to be alone, that he meant to kill the fire flickering bright between them. "I'll come in with you," she said with swift insistence.

He looked at her, his eyes black in the darkness.

"No," he said.

She wanted to argue with him, to use hot, burning words to bridge to distance he was creating. But she realized no mere language could challenge the control he was exerting. She gazed at him instead, unashamedly allowing her hunger and need and understanding to show more plainly than if she had spoken it aloud. *Please don't refuse me,* she said in silent pleading. *Love me, now.*

Desire flared bright and hard in the back of his eyes before his face closed against her. "I'll be right back," he said calmly, and she knew she had lost. She felt her heart shrivel into something so small it could easily be mistaken for a hard pebble of petrified stone, rather than a living organ. She felt her trembling cease at last, to be replaced by an icy numbness that left her blessedly free of any sensation at all. She felt her throat lock up as she said, with cool precision, "Of course."

He seemed to hesitate momentarily. Then, swearing softly, he left her, returning only when he had retrieved her case. He eased himself back into the car and turned to her. "I'm sorry," he said.

Bitterness rose like bile in her throat. "I've heard that before," she said, clutching the case against her breast. "Please, may we just go?"

"Jeri..." he began.

"And no glib explanations," she said harshly, "about how all of this is for my own good. You don't have to protect my innocence, Carter. I'm sure I'll find someone out there who will not be so... damned chivalrous."

"Jeri..."

"Just take me back to Giff's," she said, turning on him with sudden vehemence.

His hand reached out and pulled her case away from her, and she felt suddenly naked without its shielding presence.

In a quick, rough movement, he threw it in the small space behind her seat.

"Jeri, listen to me. I want to tell you about Helen."

For a moment she was absolutely still. Then, "Helen? Your fiancée?"

"My ex-fiancée," he corrected grimly.

She was silent then, waiting, wondering what new pain would follow any revelations he might make.

"Helen was the most beautiful woman I had ever known."

Oh, thanks a million, Carter, she thought. *That, of course, explains everything.*

"I was always crazy about her, even before we started seeing each other. As I told you, we had known each other for years. Hell, even our parents were close friends." She watched him run a hand through his hair, saw him as he turned from her to stare into the night shadows outside the car. "We were both nineteen when we started going out, and we stayed with each other for six years. We became a habit, I think, more than anything else. And, after a while, it seemed the most natural thing in the world to ease our sexual need with each other, too."

He paused, and she knew he was far from her in that moment, wrapped in memories she could never share. *Damn her,* she thought. *Damn her that even her memory can take him so far from me.*

He laughed raggedly, and the low sound was filled with such despair that she felt a momentary softening. *He still loves her,* she thought, thrusting aside the sudden urge she felt to reach out and comfort him.

"We were insatiable, both of us. Every conversation led to lovers' verbal foreplay, every date ended with us in bed." He paused, his hand beating a rough tattoo against his steering wheel. "I was devastated when she called off our engagement."

"Why did she..." Jeri stopped, not meaning to speak cruelly, not meaning to speak at all.

"Dump me?" he continued the thought for her. "Because...because I wanted more than just...sex. I guess it turned out that I wanted more than Helen had to offer, or wanted to commit to, anyway. After all that time, we hardly knew each other, after all."

"I don't understand."

"I wanted permanence, vows, a future. I thought she did, too."

"But she didn't?"

"Apparently not." He looked at her, and she could see in the light from the clear starlit night that his eyes were haunted. "Helen wanted to continue as we were, indefinitely, without marriage. She could pursue her own career that way, unimpeded. She had become a television announcer in Detroit, with ambitions of being a national news anchor."

"And you did not want that for her?" Jeri asked, unable to hide the accusation in her tone.

He laughed bitterly, his hand gripping the steering wheel with fierce strength. "I don't know, Jeri. I swear I didn't want to stifle her, but she made me feel...in the end, I just felt like a prize stud. And then she got pregnant."

The grief in his voice was raw, an unhealed wound laid cruelly bare for her to see. She knew the truth before he told her. "She had an abortion, didn't she?" Jeri said quietly.

For a moment she thought he would not continue. When he did, she heard in his voice a pain so profound she thought she must surely weep. "Yes. I didn't even know she was pregnant, and I heard about the abortion from a mutual friend."

Outside, in Joshua's yard, Jeri could see the shadows of the trees dark against the bright moonlight. All is shadow, she thought. Nothing is clear anymore. Only shadows of understanding, making us all feel lost and desolate and alone.

"Why are you telling me this?" she asked at last.

His hand reached out for hers, raising her palm so that she was cupping his cheek. Turning his head slightly, he kissed her palm.

"I have been celibate as a priest for the last five years, Jeri."

"But everyone says—"

"So they do," he said in wry agreement. "The funny thing is, I've done absolutely nothing to earn my undoubtedly vivid reputation. I've just built my business, kept myself busy, and lived pretty much to myself." He paused. "And watched you, Jeri."

Her hand still lay against his face. She was mildly surprised to feel the beginnings of a stubble there. She put her fingertips against his lips. He took a suddenly deep breath, expelling it softly against the soft pads of her fingers.

She lowered her hand to rest it against his thigh. He covered it with his own.

"Ah, Jeri," he said. "It feels so good to be with you. I feel right when I'm with you."

Yes, she thought. I feel whole, too. "There are ways to prevent..." she begun awkwardly.

"So there are," he agreed solemnly. "But how do you prevent betrayal, Jeri? How do you give back innocence and trust? How do you mend a broken heart?"

"I..."

"I won't take your innocence, no matter how trustingly you offer it to me, Jeri. I want to be a man, not an animal

rutting and breeding without thought of time or consequences.''

She was silent, feeling the strength of his sinews under her
hand.

"That baby gave its life because of me, Jeri," he said at
last. "The least I can do is give back a man who knows how
to choose. That is my freedom, and my prison."

"I know nothing of moral certainties," she said with her
own swift intensity. "But I know that I choose you. Please
let me choose you, Joshua."

She felt his muscles tense beneath her hand. "Do you?"
he asked flatly. "For how long? A day? A month? A year?
I won't be the initiator of pleasure in your life, only to hand
you to some other man, to watch him reap the harvest of
what I have sowed."

"Fat chance of that, Carter. You're talking to me,
Adams, the furnace repairman, remember? What other man
has ever looked at me and wanted... anything?" Jeri
laughed harshly. "What do you want from me, Joshua?"

"Why, that's easy," he said, and she could see him smiling briefly. "I wasn't going to mention this quite so soon,
but I want to marry you, Miss Adams. Will you, please?"

Later, she would find no explanation for her tears. They
came out of nowhere, blinding her with their hot sorrow.
She covered her face with her hands, wishing she could hide
from him altogether.

"Jeri," he said, and cursing the bucket seats of his sports
car, leaped out his door to suddenly appear by her side,
pulling her up, out of the car, into his arms. He led her into
the foyer just inside his front door. Wrapping his arms
around her, he let her cry against his shoulder. Smoothing
his hand down her back, he attempted to still her wildly
shaking body. "Jeri," he said again, and she thought that

never in her life would she forget the sound of his voice, saying her name.

Then his hand was curling around her neck. "I'm going to kiss you, I'm afraid," he said, and then he did, his lips warm and newly familiar against her own. She hiccuped against him, and he laughed lightly. "I do want you," he said against her open mouth. "I have imagined you a thousand times, lying beneath me, your green cat's eyes glittering in passion. I have imagined the feel of your skin against mine, and it has been the sweetest torment I have ever known. But I won't take you, not without promises and commitments and loyalties. Do you understand that?"

"Yes," she said. "No," she added. "You're not being fair," she finished helplessly.

But her words were lost into a mouth that was hot and hungry against hers, as if he were drinking at a fountain where the sweet water had been too long awaited. He held her coat tightly closed between them, as if he feared his own control, after all. And when he was done, she said with childlike anger, "If I, in my inexperience, feel this strongly, how will you be able to resist, Carter? I may want more, too. Will it be your right to make my choices for me?"

His hand brushed her cheek and came away moist from her tears. "I have the responsibility for my own decisions, not yours," he said. "But when you choose me, you choose my choices also."

"I choose nothing!" she cried, desperate to the last. "I don't have your experience or your understanding. I am sorry about your baby, Joshua, but I could care less about your damn self-centered fiancée! I never wanted a knight in shining armor. I just want you to love me, Carter. I never thought any man would want to...would want me. Please love me, Joshua. Tonight. Please."

But her coat was still buttoned up tight, and his arms were around her shoulders, leading her back out to his car.

"And therein lies the thorny problem, Jeri," he said with wry acceptance. "God help me, I do love you."

His next words came as a whisper of winter breeze, brushing against the walls that were crumbling around her heart. "But it's you, Jeri, who holds the final answer. For it's you who will have to do the choosing."

Chapter Eight

She had come to Giff as a toddler with nothing more than the clothes on her back. She had not been a pretty child; Daniel had never really known how to care for the little girl entrusted to his care. Her hair was wild and tangled, her arms and legs poking like thin sticks out of too-small night-clothes, her face pinched and wary. She was clutching a Raggedy Ann doll someone had thrust into her arms after the fire, it was almost as big as she was. She could remember nothing of the night in which her father was killed by the fire, and she had no memories at all of her mother. Giff became her one stable anchor in a world that had been confused and lonely for a long time. She had practically deified him with her worship. She would do whatever he asked, with the air of a young puppy whose tail is wagging so hard he almost loses his balance from its wild beating. As she got older, there were only two things she denied Giff: she refused to cut her hair, and she would not give up the doll that continued to be the one constant friend in her lonely, isolated childhood.

Jeri was holding that doll now as she stood looking out her bedroom window. She could see the frozen inland lake glinting silver blue in the late afternoon sun. Happy that tomorrow was the first of February, and winter was just that much closer to being over, she watched a white-tailed rabbit run across Giff's yard, pausing momentarily at the edge of the lake as if deciding in which direction to go.

Choices. She had made so very few. Mainly she had just adapted—to being an orphan, to pleasing Giff, to being alone. In fact, before she had told Giff that she was staying with Joshua last Tuesday morning, she could not remember making a single independent choice in her entire life.

The rabbit had turned to the left, and she watched until it was hidden in the trees and underbrush that separated Giff's neat, well-manicured yard from the wildly tangled natural forest beyond.

Opposites. Joshua had asked her to choose. He wanted her to leave Giff, to marry him. Her expression was bitter as she realized that leaving Giff should be the easiest thing of all. Unfortunately the opposite was true. Giff had been her tree of life for as long as she could remember; she had lived all her days in the shade of his twisted branches. She feared she had no idea how to survive in the heat of the sun. And to leave Giff only to walk straight into the life of a man whom, she reminded herself, she barely knew? To marry him? She didn't think she had enough trust in her entire soul to make such a commitment.

Rubbing her arms absently, she watched as storm clouds gathered over the lake, blocking the light of the sun.

She wondered if she was doomed forever to live only as the reflection seen in a man's eyes. She walked to her dresser, to examine herself in the mirror there. Her hand brushed lightly against the head of her Raggedy Ann doll, which smiled vacantly at her from its reflection in the mirror.

But if she was so doomed, which reflection would she choose? Upon what basis would she decide? Abruptly she pulled the doll to her breast, wrapping her arms around it and herself. She lowered her head and brushed her cheek against the doll's coarse hair.

Joshua's demands were unfair, she told herself. Even she knew one week of intensity such as she and Joshua had just shared did not necessarily guarantee a lifetime commitment.

I have wanted you for a long time, he had said.

She sat on the edge of her bed, still clutching her old friend. She felt herself beginning to grow warm, soft. *Married.* It was all so unbelievable.

He was every woman's dream man, she reminded herself. *And he wants you. By some miracle, some illogical gift of fate, he wants you. He wants to marry you. If you turn him down, you will never in a million years get another proposal as good as this one. No matter what his reasons, what his illusions or his needs, he is the finest prospect you are ever likely to have.*

Deliberately she turned and dropped the doll between the two pillows atop her bed, then sat with her head in her hands. *I don't know who I am,* she thought. *I don't know why I'm here or what I want to do with my life. Surely it would be wrong for me to marry Joshua when I don't even know myself.* The unspoken thoughts came to her quickly, in a still, small voice that she could hear only with her heart. And then she knew: these were the true questions, and they came, not from Giff, not from Joshua, but from her own soul. *Who am I?* she cried silently. *What good am I?* She remembered her joy after her accident, the realization that she had been given a second chance to do something with her own life.

I don't know who I am, she told herself over and over. I am a stranger to myself.

The inner voice spoke, more strongly this time. Find out, it said. It's your birthright, the same as for every child born.

And she understood, at last, the choice. She could continue forever, adapting, reacting, sliding through life. Or she could discover who she really was, could acknowledge her own accountability to herself.

It was then that she began to weep, sobbing quietly as great silent tears rolled down her cheeks. She cried for her lost, stolen childhood. She cried for the adolescent girl who had been forced to deny her own tentative sexuality. She cried for the woman whose walls had been so thick and hard that it had taken a true Joshua to tear them down.

When she was done, she found that her decisions had made themselves. She knew that eventually she was going to have to leave Giff. Yet she understood that she was not ready to promise Joshua anything. And she knew that never again would she abdicate her responsibility for her own destiny. For, in her grief and desolation, she had emerged from her own refiner's fire, made stronger and purer and brighter in the heat of her own life's burning flame.

The next day was Monday and Jeri went out on her service calls. She drove the new van Giff had purchased. He had handed her the keys without a word, and she had discovered that the new service vehicle was already stocked with tools—some new, some salvaged from her wreck. So quickly life returns to normal, she thought. Only I have changed, and all the scars are invisible.

Monday night she called Joshua.

"I'll come this Friday to decorate your house," she told him. "And every Friday from now on."

"That's great," he said, sounding pleased. "But Friday is a long way off. I want to see you before then."

"No," she said too quickly. "No."

A pause, then, "Why not, Jeri?"

How could she explain the feeling she had of newness, of fragile self-identity? How could she tell him that he terrified her, that she feared the almost drugging need she felt every time he was near? She would not even try. "I don't want to see you before then, Joshua," she said instead, bluntly. "I don't want you to call me. I have too many things to sort out."

Silence. She wondered if she had been too harsh, if she could have softened her words, offered better explanations. Then he spoke. "But you will come for sure, Jeri?"

She took a deep breath. "I'll be there Friday morning, Joshua. Nine o'clock."

"I'll come and get you," he said quickly.

"No, thank you. I think I can manage to drive myself."

"Well," he said. "All right then."

"Yes, all right," she repeated inanely. "Goodbye, Joshua."

"Jeri?"

"What?"

"Have you been kissing any other men?"

The question unnerved her, reminding her of needs and hungers simmering just under the surface of their relationship.

"No," she whispered, her fingers flying up to touch her lips briefly.

"Good," he said, and she could see his crooked smile as clearly as if he were there in the kitchen with her. "Just keep it that way," he said. "I'll see you Friday, babe."

After the phone call, Jeri went into the living room where Giff was drinking beer and watching some late night television program. On impulse, she went to sit beside him on the sofa.

For some time they watched together in silence. She remembered other times when she had sat, just like this, watching television with Giff, neither speaking nor touching, just wanting to be with him, wanting him to acknowledge her, to love her.

The program ended. Giff pushed the remote control button that turned off the television. Before he could rise and leave her, Jeri said quickly, "Can we talk, Giff?"

For a moment she thought he was going to ignore her, shrug her off. But then he relaxed and sat back into the sofa. His hand began to play with the buttons of the television remote, without actually pressing any. He was not looking at her.

"I'm going to be taking Fridays and Saturdays off from now on, Giff."

He immediately tensed, and his hand stilled against the sofa arm.

"Joshua has asked me to decorate his house for him," she said, not bothering to mask the sudden pride that had crept into her voice. *How much I have hidden from you,* she thought. *But no more, Giff. I'm not hiding any more.* "I'm going to spend every Friday doing it."

"What about Saturdays?" Giff asked in a tone of deceptive mildness.

"Saturdays will be my own."

Giff did not move, but somehow the silence emanating from his expressionless visage became thick with suppressed fury. She watched his hand grip the fabric of the sofa.

"I can't spare you, Jeraldine," he said. "Not at this time of year. You know that. Maybe in the summer—"

"And maybe when hell freezes over, Giff," she interrupted with swift intensity. "I'll be twenty-five this August. All my life I have been keeping your house, making your meals, doing your laundry. Since my sixteenth birthday I've been working in your business, putting in long hours, turning myself as best I could into a son for you. It's crazy, isn't it? I'm both wife and son to you, but what am I to me, Giff? What am I to me?"

Her low voice faded away, and she wondered that she had even tried to reach this man as his hands steepled sharply and he said, "I find it absolutely amazing that you have never had these self-doubts before," he said. "This is absurd, Jeraldine. I can't put you on a four-day schedule, not at this time of year. What you really need more than time off is to tell that bastard to leave you alone."

"I won't do that, Giff," she said, keeping her voice low and smooth even as her heart began to pump erratically.

"Well, then, who do you suggest will do your work while you're off playing lover-girl with Carter?"

"I explained to you, Giff. I'm going to be decorating his house, nothing else. And Saturdays will be my own."

He snorted derisively. "And who did you say would do your work during this totally useless voyage of self-discovery?" Giff's voice was sarcastic, sneering, and she stood abruptly at his tone.

"I don't know, and I don't care," she said fiercely. "All I know is, I am taking Fridays and Saturdays off from now on."

He stood also. In his stocking feet, he was only fractionally taller then Jeri, and she met his furious glare evenly. "I could fire you, you know," he said softly.

She stared at him, registering the threat, and realized with a totally unexpected relief that at this moment she had no fear of him, not of his words, nor of his rejection, therefore he had no power over her. She almost smiled in her sudden triumph. As he studied her face, his expression changed, became infinitely more subtle.

"He really has you where he wants you, doesn't he?" Giff said. "How does it feel to be Joshua Carter's new toy, Jeraldine?"

She sucked in her breath sharply as she absorbed his poisonous cruelty. "I'm no one's toy," she said with quiet dignity. "Not even yours, Giff. Not even yours."

The rest of the week passed in a haze for Jeri. The peace she had felt earlier had left her, leaving a rending pain behind that made her confused and withdrawn. Once, while driving to a job, she had seen a great old tree lying on its side by the road, its roots upended, a violent reminder of the storm the night Joshua had spent in Giff's house. She found herself crying for no reason.

Giff's anger grew in direct proportion to her quiet distance from him. He gave her impossibly difficult work schedules—she worked hard and late, not finishing her days until long past ten. On Wednesday it was midnight before she walked through Giff's door, exhausted and filthy and raging in anger. But he was already in bed; by morning she had cooled down enough to say nothing.

In fact, she spoke to Giff as little as possible, and she was barely civil to her customers. Their constant comments about Giff's popularity and generosity met with a stony-eyed response; she knew she was fueling the rumor mills for months to come. She stayed away from Bill's Tavern and from anywhere else she might meet anyone she knew.

At night she continued to have nightmares, and they were getting worse. Tired as she was, she was getting to the point where she dreaded going to bed. Every night she woke sweating and shaking, and she knew she was going slowly crazy. Joshua consumed her. A totally irrational guilt about Giff consumed her. Her own fears consumed her. Finally she took to pulling her ancient Raggedy Ann doll off her dresser and sleeping with it in her arms.

But the momentum of her changing did not slow. On Wednesday she had lunch with Susan. On Thursday she defied Giff's sadistic schedule and once again went shopping. And on Friday she returned to the house that Joshua had built.

By the time she reached Joshua's home on Friday morning, she had herself well in hand. If she would never again throw herself at Joshua, begging him to ease the need he had planted in her, she would also refuse to listen to any more proposals of marriage. She would not be rushed into a decision she was not prepared to make, and she would not allow Joshua to be the only one deciding the parameters of their relationship. She had formulated some demands of her own that she would state to him clearly and calmly. And she would take at face value Joshua's request for help with decorating his home; she would be brisk and businesslike, attacking the task with the same professional calm she used on her furnace jobs.

Joshua's front door opened before she even had a chance to knock, and she knew he had been waiting for her. "Hi, babe," he said, softly, before pulling her inside. She barely had an opportunity to register his informal clothing of jeans and red flannel shirt before she was in his arms and his mouth was covering her own.

She had thought they would kiss again, before the day was over, but she had not expected it to be so soon, before she even had a chance to say anything. She clung to her good intentions even as she clung to him for support.

Eventually he let her go, putting her away from him. Gently he took the case she was carrying and dropped it to the floor. Slowly, deliberately, he began to undo the buttons of her new coat. Nervously she tried to slap his fingers away. "I can do it myself, Carter," she said.

"But I want to," he said gently, removing her hands and directing them to her side. "Hold still, Jeri." He began to work on the second button.

The lassitude, which was becoming an all too familiar characteristic when she was in Joshua's presence, began to overpower her. She watched him helplessly as his sure, strong fingers managed the fastenings, as he was forced to kneel in front of her to reach the lowest buttons. At last he was finished, and she stood still and silent before his kneeling figure, her coat hanging open.

He rose, sliding his hands inside her coat, brushing the sides of her body as his arms moved to surround her. "I shouldn't be doing this," he murmured. "I promised myself I wouldn't touch you." Slowly he drew her coat down off her shoulders until it dropped with her case onto the floor.

She was wearing a pencil straight skirt with an oversized sweatshirt that hung below her hips, both in royal blue. Her hair swung free and easy, a simple barrette pulling it back from her eyes. Joshua cupped her face with his hands and kissed her, so softly, so gently. *Trust me,* the kiss said. "You're beautiful," he said.

He drew her body to his, deepening his kiss as he did so. She remembered how close they had been on the dance floor last Saturday night, and it was like that now, only there was no music except that which his hands and mouth were making. When at last his lips lifted from hers, she whispered, "What are you doing to me?"

"The same thing you are doing to me, I think," he said, watching her carefully. Some of her confusion and repressed anger must have shown there, because he sighed. "Still don't trust me, do you Jeri?" he said, before adding, "Have you had breakfast?" almost whimsically. At her short, negative nod, he took her hand and led her to his bedroom. He had laid out a plate of bagels, cheese, and jellies on his small worktable, and the smell of hot, fresh coffee filled the room. Swiftly she moved to sit down, taking a bagel in one hand as she did so.

"I came to help with your house," she said, her voice stiff in spite of all her best efforts. "I don't want anything more, Joshua." Then she added, wanting to make sure he understood perfectly. "I don't want you to touch me anymore."

He had followed her across his room, was just now lowering himself into a chair opposite her as she spoke. His eyes narrowed slightly at her words, and at first he said nothing. She watched in some apprehension as he spread cream cheese and jelly on a bagel of his own. Finally he met her stare evenly, saying with a small shrug, "If that is what you want, Jeri."

"It confuses me," she said, "and I am confused enough already." She saw warm understanding in his eyes, and she felt herself relax. She knew that with those few words, she had begun her own declaration of independence. I can act as well as be acted upon, she thought. If I lose Joshua over this, then he is not what I want at all.

The first hours of the day were spent going over Joshua's house in minute detail. Jeri took meticulous notes on measurements, electrical outlets, windows, doorways. He freely answered any questions she had, and she felt anew the respect she had for his work.

He took her to lunch in Traverse City, and over the soup and sandwiches they ordered she spoke to him frankly. "I don't understand you, at all," she said. "Why aren't you an architect in your own right? When you can create something as beautiful as your home, how can you be happy doing anything else?"

Joshua shrugged. "I like what I do. I see no reason to make a change. I know who I am, and what I want."

How nice, Jeri thought, to know who you are and be comfortable with it.

Later, as they rose to leave, her eyes wandered to a table across the room. For the first time she noticed that two high school acquaintances, long since married, were sitting there, talking with each other with great animation. Two toddlers sat at the table with them, and one of the women was running her fingers fondly through a child's hair. The sight held her momentarily motionless as a strange yearning filled her breast. It was all she had never known—childhood and motherhood, friendship and trust, and the hunger she felt must have been written clearly in her eyes, because when she jerked around to smile brightly at Joshua, his own expression contained such tenderness that any words she might have spoken died in her throat.

"Come," he said softly, holding out her coat. He had kept his hands from her all morning, but now as he helped her into her coat, his hands tightened around her arms. "We could make a baby of our own, Jeri," he whispered in her ear, and she knew that he was again seducing her with his terrible knowledge.

Afterward they began roaming the stores. Jeri meant for Joshua to purchase several area rugs, along with a couple of major pieces of furniture. But her constant awareness of his presence at her side made her feel vague and uncertain, and the day ended with no purchases made. He took her out for dinner, commenting laughingly. "Perhaps we ought to concentrate on my kitchen. It would be nice to have a real meal at home."

Later, he asked, "Do you have to go right back to Giff's? Would you stay with me for a little while?"

And she thought of the case he had dropped on the foyer floor earlier that morning. "I can stay with you," she said quietly.

He lit a fire in his bedroom fireplace and sat across from her in one of his matched wing chairs, his stockinged feet stretching across the space between them to rest on her lap. "It's not touching, precisely." He grinned at her, and she forced herself to smile back, even though the weight of his feet atop her thighs was yet a new intimacy for which she was unprepared. He had placed a cassette of lyrical folk tunes in his tape recorder, and for a while they sat, speaking desultorily of unimportant matters, and for once Jeri felt at home with the silences that seemed to flow like soothing music around Joshua, and that brushed off on her a little, too. She leaned back into her chair, her defenses completely gone. Her body was fluid, her heart at peace. Unconsciously she had been rubbing one of Joshua's feet; she did not notice when his face grew still and his eyes dark, until an involuntary noise escaped his throat, and her eyes met his in a moment of electrical intensity. She realized what she had been doing and flushed lightly.

"Excuse me," he said, and rose from his chair. "I have some work I could do, if you don't mind." She knew he was seeking distraction as he seated himself at his table, pulling out some architectural drawings and unrolling them with quick, sure movements.

"Do you want me to leave?" she asked.

"No," he said. "I want to make love to you."

How was she supposed to respond to that? Especially when he continued, his voice low and rasping, "But I won't."

"I really should leave," she said.

"No," he said harshly. "Stay. Just a while longer."

Casting about in her mind for something to talk about, she recalled that except for their short conversation at lunchtime, he had not once spoken of his construction business, nor had its demands made any encroachment on his life.

"What about your business, Joshua?" she asked him. "Will you be able to spend every Friday with me?"

His eyes sliced around to meet hers. "No problem," he said briefly.

"But you own it . . . I would think you have to be there."

"I have men out on six sites right now, each with a very capable foreman. I have an office with three employees. My manager is a very competent woman who raised eight children before she came to work for me. She can handle practically anything that comes up in my absence. And, if all else fails, I'm only a phone call away."

"You've done this in just the five years you've been in Traverse City?" she queried with amazement in her tone.

"Yeah. I did it. In five years." His eyes glittered, and she remembered his lost baby.

She was silent then, sitting for long moments with her feet curled up beneath her, while Joshua pretended to work at his table. After a while she knew the pretense had ended and he was concentrating in earnest on the huge pieces of vellum in front of him, and her eyes grew heavy and she slept.

The fire had burned to low flames when she awoke, stretching a neck that had stiffened from her odd sitting position. Slowly she uncurled her legs.

Joshua was again sitting across from her, watching her with eyes shadowed dark by the flickering light of the fireplace.

"I didn't mean to fall asleep," she said.

"It didn't matter. I enjoyed watching you."

"What time is it?"

"Almost midnight," he told her gravely.

"I suppose I really must go."

There was an almost imperceptible pause before he said, "Yes."

She thought of her room at the end of the hall in Giff's house. She remembered how she had slept with her ancient doll in her arms every night this week. She remembered the terror of her nightmares.

Her eyelashes swept down on her cheek, hiding her eyes, as she reluctantly rose from her chair. Some of her hair had fallen forward so that it hung across her breast, and she noticed it was tangled. Using her fingers, she began to separate the strands.

"Do you have a brush, Jeri?"

Her eyes flew up to meet his. "You mean with me? Here?"

He nodded, his eyes never leaving hers.

"I have one in my bag," she said softly.

"Will you let me brush your hair before you go?"

She got the brush from her purse, and he sat her in one of the chairs at the small table and gently began brushing her hair. Ten minutes passed, then twenty. His strokes were slow, mesmerizing and she thought, how many ways he knows to give pleasure. At last the brush was still and her head was back against his body. She could feel the tightness and hardness held in check there.

"Would you like me to stay?" she asked him.

She watched in the mirrored wall when he closed his eyes as if against a sudden pain. His hand clenched in her hair. "Yes," he said flatly. "More than you know."

Her hand reached up to encircle his. "Giff is so angry with me," she said. "And I have been having the most terrible dreams."

She felt him sigh. "Do you really want to stay with me?"

For a long moment she did not say anything. "I don't know," she said at last, her voice small and uncertain. "But I don't want to go back to Giff's, Joshua."

"You will have to face him sometime, Jeri."

She knew that, of course. But right now she did not want to return to her room at the end of the hallway in Giff's house. Anything was better than returning to that dark place, where nightmares haunted her and Giff remained so unpleasantly condemning. So she was silent.

He pulled her out of the chair and onto the bed, where he could sit beside her and put his arms around her and pull her head down onto his chest. She knew she had lost control again. She probably ought to be filled with anger, if not at Joshua, then certainly at herself. But, instead, what she felt was a deep peace. *I am safe here,* she thought. *Here is home.* And after a while, she felt drowsy again, and she closed her eyes, giving in to sleep willingly.

As if from a great distance, she heard Joshua talking. "If you leave your car here, I could drive you home."

No. That didn't sound very appealing at all. She shifted in his arms. "Please," she said. "Let me stay here with you."

She felt his immediate tension; it communicated itself to her through every place where their bodies touched. She was afraid she had made him angry.

"I won't ask you to do anything," she assured him huskily. "I won't even sleep with you. I'll stay in a chair, all night. Just don't make me go back to Giff's, please."

"That bastard," he said, his voice low. "What has he done to you, honey?"

She shrugged helplessly. "He's furious with me," she said inadequately, not wanting to explain all the many ways he had made her life miserable over the past few days. Giff seemed far away now, and she had no desire to bring him closer.

"He'll be angrier still if you stay here with me."

"Impossible," she said, not caring.

She could almost hear him thinking, testing his own strength against the temptation the coming night would provide.

"All right. You can spend the night here."

She relaxed against him in sleepy relief. His hand began to rub her arm, gently. She felt suspended, lost in a place where everything was new, where the past could be forgotten forever. But she was so incredibly tired. She wondered if it was her lack of sleep that was making her so exhausted now. Her eyes fluttered shut.

Sometime later Joshua's voice awakened her. "As I see it, Jeri, we've got two choices," he was saying.

"What?" she mumbled against his shirt front.

"We can do the honorable thing and I can sleep on the floor, or we could do what would be really nice and spend the night in each other's arms."

She lay against his chest, waiting for him to decide, unsurprised that he had not taken seriously her willingness to spend the night in his chair.

"What will it be, honey?"

So. He was making her choose. She laughed shakily. For her, who had never been held or stroked in her life, this was no choice at all. "I would like to sleep with you, Joshua."

He sighed. "I asked for it, I guess. And only I know what we're really missing."

She smiled but lay still in his arms.

"I suppose you didn't bring a nightgown?" he asked dryly.

"No."

"Well, you're going to have to go the bathroom and make whatever changes you want to make. The last thing I want to have to do is undress you myself."

Still in her beautiful, empty, suspended state of mind, she stumbled to her feet. Grasping her overnight bag, she went to the adjoining bathroom. Forcing herself to take a quick shower, she dressed hurriedly again in her huge oversized sweatshirt. Suddenly overcome with shyness, she gazed at herself in the mirror. "What are you doing, Adams?" she asked herself aloud. "You have got to be one hundred percent crazy." She slowly entered Joshua's room. He gazed at her frankly, his blue eyes traveling the length of her body, absorbing the impact of her slender legs peeking out from underneath her long shirt. Her hair, made fluffy from the dampness of the shower, hung over her shoulders and surrounded her face like a cloud.

"You look like a princess," he said.

She smiled and moved to get into his bed. "Your turn for the bathroom," she said.

He was back in minutes, but she was already drifting into sleep. She did not question it when he pulled her against his body, clad only in pajama bottoms. She felt his hand take an exploratory trip down the length of her, from her shoulder to her knees.

He cleared his throat. "Just as a matter of scientific inquiry," he said. "What are you wearing underneath this thing?"

"Nothing," she answered, barely awake.

"Ah, Jeri," he said. Then, "Go to sleep, honey."

And she did.

Jeri did not return to Giff's all that weekend. Every time she thought about returning to Giff, some force, heavy and dark and fearful, settled on her. In the end she simply did not go.

She spent all day Saturday with Joshua, going through antique shops, stopping at carpet stores, browsing in the same furniture stores they had visited the day before. This time they did make some purchases—chairs and a table for Joshua's kitchen, plates and pans and cutlery for the cabinets. They decided to cook dinner that very night. So then they had to go grocery shopping, and they performed the ordinary task with their arms linked in easy companionship.

They laughed more than Jeri knew was ever possible, and freely touched and gazed and smiled at each other. Later, when they lay together in Joshua's big warm water bed, he held her close and spoke to her in private words of hunger and desire and love. He told her of waiting, of uncertainty, of joy that she was finally with him. And he asked her again to marry him.

But she could not give him the answer he wanted, even though their bodies tangled around each other in sleep, for that night, and the night after.

Monday morning she left him to return to Giff's.

Chapter Nine

Giff had a small summer boathouse down by the dock. In the summer Jeri had spent many hours in its sandy shade; it had been her favorite place. It was here she brought her Raggedy Ann doll, here that she had spun all her childhood fantasies. Tales of mother and father, sisters and brothers interwined with all her imaginary games. But the most potent dream of all had been that of her own private prince, who had seen through her outer shell to the loving girl beneath. He came in many forms—sometimes tall and dark, sometimes fair and slim—but he always came. Of course she had long ago outgrown such ridiculous pretenses, but the spot by the boathouse still held a special place in her heart.

It was that piece of ground that occupied her mind now as she drove her pickup through the light snowfall into Giff's driveway. She could tell from the lights shining through the windows of Giff's office that he was already there, even though it was just seven-thirty. Business as usual, she thought, and then wished with all her heart that it could be so.

It took no special intuition to know that Giff would be furious that she had stayed away for the entire weekend, and she had been struggling with various explanations since leaving Joshua's house. It was a foregone conclusion that Giff would put the worst possible interpretation upon her extended absence. There was no way Giff would believe in white knights—she would not even bother to attempt to persuade him that her virtue was still intact.

As if it should matter, she told herself firmly. I'm twenty-four. I deserve a life of my own.

Still, by the time she entered Giff's home she had worked herself into a frenzy of guilty, miserable anxiety. The temperature outside had dropped; she felt the warmth of Giff's house envelop her like a thick, smothering blanket. Closing the mudroom door behind her as she entered the kitchen, she leaned against it, trying to calm herself by taking deep breaths as her eyes slowly focused on the well-known spaces.

It seemed a lifetime had passed since she had last passed through these doors. She had to remind herself that in reality only three days had elapsed. As she walked through the rooms, she gazed at the home where she had been raised, as if seeing it for the first time. It was a luxury dwelling by the standards of those in the surrounding communities, yet after the brightness and light of Joshua's house, this one felt dark and cloistered to her.

She stood in the center of Giff's living room, acknowledging with bitter self-acceptance that no matter how much she had tried to lighten the atmosphere of this place, coming back to it had always made her feel heavy, less alive, as if the house were a black hole of darkness, sucking her into itself and absorbing her identity in its shadowed corners.

She returned to the kitchen, pausing momentarily to inspect a decorative straw hat she had hung on an inside wall years ago. Its crown was adorned with pink and white silk flowers; a wide rose ribbon dangled gracefully from its brim. She smiled, remembering when she had purchased the hat at a local craft show. She had not been able to resist its blatant romanticism.

Now her hand stilled where it had reached out to lightly fondle the ribbon. She had surrounded the hat with a variety of small, old, gardening tools, and the blade of each tool was directed toward the soft rounded curve of the ultra-feminine hat.

Something came together in her mind, some key of knowledge turning in a door that had been previously locked to her. Disbelieving, she turned and faced the room, noting other similarities for the first time. The round oak table was there, surrounded by the most uncompromising straight-backed chairs. She remembered Joshua commenting on their Shaker lines. But Shakers never believed in procreation; they were a whole society of men and women who lived absolutely separate from each other. No wonder they had died out, she told herself wryly. And I sit every day in their chairs.

A ceramic cow, her udders almost comically full and heavy, was placed next to a replica of a miniature branding iron. She laughed silently to herself. I announced my need to anyone who cared to look, she thought. Everywhere is softness surrounded, fenced in, wounded. Everywhere is womanhood denied. The most sacred secrets of my heart are laid open before the world.

Her hands clenched and unclenched, and she took deep painful breaths as she acknowledged her torment, so long entombed behind these walls. Joshua, she thought. Did you see it all and love me still? Yet there is no answering love in me, to give back to you in full measure. I have been damaged too long. There is no healing for such a one as me.

She walked to her bedroom, closing the door tightly behind her. Even here, with her old doll grinning sightlessly at her from the dresser, she felt a sudden, unwelcome stranger. She threw her coat on the bed. Her attention was caught by the image that was reflected in the mirror.

She was still wearing the royal skirt and oversized sweatshirt she had donned on Friday morning. She had borrowed Joshua's washer yesterday and laundered everything, wrapping herself temporarily in his big, roomy robe. She remembered the way he stared at her, his eyes following her with a yearning insistence as she had moved about his house, naked except for the covering he had given her.

Still in awe of the power of her newly discovered sexuality, she had been unable to resist flaunting herself before him, leaning over so that he could see the curve of her bare breasts, turning quickly so that the closure of the robe flapped opened, fondling the lapels of the robe with sensuous slowness, her fingertips touching her own bare skin underneath. She had found the resulting tension that grew between them to be a wonderfully heady experience until Joshua had become abruptly angry and stormed out into the snow, leaving her alone with a dawning sense of shame and a curiously empty ache. When he returned, she had been dressed, and she had not attempted to tease him again.

Yet his anger had been gone when he had come back to her. It had been replaced by a kind of tortured resignation, a haunted hunger that had made her want to weep.

How little I really know, she thought. If I live to be a hundred, I will never understand Joshua Carter.

Now she stripped out of her new finery and pulled some old jeans and a workshirt from her closet. Her fingers shook while she zipped up the jeans and fumbled at the buttons of her shirt. Braiding her hair with deliberately swift movements, she faced her reflection once more, hard defiance sparking her eyes. This was a person she recognized. This was the person who belonged in this room, in this house. And this was the person who was going to have to face Giff.

She found him in his office when she entered it just a little past eight o'clock. She was unhappily surprised to find Bob Pritchett there, lounging in a chair by Giff's desk with a familiar ease that sent warning goose bumps prickling down Jeri's neck. She assumed the two other men who worked for Giff had already been and left. Giff was a stickler for early starts, and she knew he paid just well enough to ensure that his men responded to his wishes.

Pritchett's tall, lanky form was folded into his chair, one long leg crossed over the other, as he looked over his day's schedule. His left eye still showed some discoloration from the punch Joshua had given him at the tavern two weeks ago. He looked up at her as she entered, and his knowing leer was all she needed to tell her that Giff had been speaking of where she had been the last three days.

Giff himself was seated at his desk, scribbling notes on a job sheet. She was sure he was aware of her presence; she had the distinctly uncomfortable sensation of being purposely ignored. She stood calmly, refusing to reveal either her unease or her rising anger.

Giff laid his ink pen down, swiveled his chair around slightly, and looked at her at last, his brown eyes bleak and cold. "Well," he said. "You decided to show up."

Jeri felt every muscle tighten as if in response to an unspoken threat. She felt the heavy, rhythmical pounding of her heart as a drum call to battle. She stood very still and very straight. Yet she was aware of an odd detachment, a curious separation of her mind from her body. She felt strangely insulated, coldly untouchable; even Giff's too-familiar domination could not reach her now. It was as if she were merely an observer here, taking unseen notes, impartially wondering what would happen next. So must a soldier feel when he goes to meet the enemy, she thought.

From behind his desk, Giff stood abruptly. His thick hair was combed neatly back, as usual. His clothing was immaculate, his bow tie precisely knotted. She watched as if from a great distance as his eyebrows pulled together to an invisible point in the middle of his forehead. His thin lips drew out in a straight, uncompromising line. His lean, aged cheeks sucked in until they formed two hollows on either side of his narrow nose. And she knew without glancing down that Giff's thin, veined hands were both being held in the curiously tight, splayed manner that was his trademark when he was angry. *Like hawk's talons,* she thought.

"May I speak to you alone, please, Giff?" she heard herself requesting quietly.

He stared at her a moment before replying, "I've got nothing private to say, Jeraldine."

Pritchett smiled.

So be it. If this was the way the game would be played, she would still play it.

"Then I would like my work list, Giff," she said.

"You would like your list," he repeated, as if she had said something wildly funny. "My, my, Jeraldine. Do you think you're going to have the energy to take care of your calls today? I'm sure your weekend was quite . . . exhausting."

I don't have to take this, she thought, and she knew that some part of her had begun a silent seething. Yet she stood there, saying nothing, carefully watching this man who had raised her, who had clothed and fed her, who had taken her in when she was an orphan.

Bob Pritchett was grinning evilly.

The silence grew as Giff waited for her response.

"*Do* you have a schedule for me, Giff?" she asked, surprising herself by the calm assurance in her tone. Surely this was someone else speaking, someone else standing so cool before the blazing heat of Giff's disapproval. "If you do, I would like it. If not, I've got plenty of things to fill my day."

"I'll just bet you do," Giff said. He met her eyes for the first time, and she was unsurprised to find undiluted hatred there. All these years you've hated me, she thought. I was trying to make you love me, but it was hopeless. With an almost invisible movement she squared her shoulders, forcing herself to meet his malevolent gaze steadily.

She no longer cared that Bob Pritchett was there, witnessing her supposed humiliation. She would say what she had come to say and be done with it. "I'm giving you my notice," she spoke evenly, almost gently. "Four weeks, Giff."

Pritchett uncrossed his legs and leaned forward, his elbows on his knees. Giff began to rock back and forth on his heels.

"Well, now," Giff said, his voice diminished to a guttural hiss. "She's gone completely crazy, Bob. A true madwoman in our midst."

Pritchett chortled derisively.

Jeri waited until Giff's expression changed. "I'm leaving you, Giff," she repeated, "in four weeks."

Giff's face turned a pasty white in the morning light. His eyes widened and grew peculiarly bright; it seemed she could see an almost bestial cruelty there. His rigidly held lips seemed like a purple slash against the abnormal whiteness of his skin.

"You can't leave me," he sneered. "I raised you, Jeraldine. I took you in when nobody wanted you. You owe me."

But the old argument was impotent in the face of her newfound strength. "You gave me food and shelter and clothing, Giff, that's all. I think you've been paid well enough for those things. You've had plenty of reimbursement, in coinage you have never understood. You've had all my loyalty and affection for as long as I can remember, Giff. I gave you the greatest gift I knew how to give. But you were unworthy of the gift. And now I'm not going to give it to you anymore."

Giff's head jerked back slightly, his nostrils flared. "You're being ridiculous," he snapped. "Joshua Carter is responsible for this... this aberration on your part. That bastard has twisted you, Jeraldine. He's using you to get at me. He's had it all planned, I know it. You're a fool if you can't see it."

Bob Pritchett was sitting very still, absorbing the argument between herself and Giff with careful intensity. Out of the corner of her eye she watched him lightly pinch his lips between his thumb and forefinger.

"Just give me my schedule, Giff," she said, feeling incredibly weary, wanting nothing so much as for this interview to be over. "I want to go to work."

Grasping a sheet of paper between his tightly clenched fingers, Giff walked with short, angry steps around his desk so that he was standing directly in front of Jeri.

"How was he, Jeraldine?" Giff asked in a tight, angry voice that she could barely recognize as belonging to him. "Did he make you moan? Did you cry out for him? What kind of a woman are you that you will bed down with the first man who looks your way?"

With such words he had wounded her before, keeping her insecure and afraid of her own being. It should have made her feel weak and miserable that he could say such things to her, that even now a part of her believed him. But she only felt old, and very tired, and quite empty.

"May I have my schedule, Giff?"

Giff thrust the sheet of paper in her hand with rough anger. "Just like your mother," he said, using his final, ultimate weapon in this battle of wills. "You're a tramp, just like your mother."

Enough was enough. Studying her list with blind eyes, she said with deceptive gentleness, "No, Giff, I'm no tramp."

She sensed his fury as it grew in direct proportion to her uncowed calmness. "You are..." he said, his voice hot with his hate, "...just like your mother."

She raised her eyes to meet his. She forgot about Bob Pritchett sitting there, lapping up this scene like a rooting pig among some favorite garbage.

"You don't know me at all, Giff," she said. "You don't know what I want or how I think. I've been full of words that nobody has ever heard, do you know that? But Joshua Carter listened, Giff. Every day of my life you've seen me speak and act and pretend, but you've never once heard me feel, Giff. It took Joshua to do that. It's him I owe, not you. Never you."

Shaking her head in blanket negation of anything Giff might say, she turned abruptly and left his office. She stepped onto the pavement, letting the door shut behind her before she raised the back of her hand to her mouth and pressed, hard. It was all she could do not to cry out, to scream her innocence and her pain. She turned toward her service van. She felt an overwhelming urge to flee, to get as far from here as she could.

As she was reaching for the handle of her van, she felt a well-muscled hand clamp down on her arm. Thinking at first that Giff had followed her, she looked up with bruised, shadowed eyes, automatically pulling her arm away. But it wasn't Giff who stood there, holding her momentarily captive. It was Bob Pritchett, smiling at her unpleasantly.

"So, Joshua Carter finally got you in his bed," he jeered at her. "Well, I don't mind, not in the least. But you sure have old man Adams going strong, don't you, Jeraldine? And all for nothing, really, because Carter will be dead tired of you before the month is out." Pritchett cackled; she recoiled from the sourness of his breath upon her face. "At least you'll be one broken-in filly when he is done with you. There's plenty of us out here that would like a taste of what he's been having."

"You disgust me, Pritchett," she said icily. "Let me go."

It was the wrong thing to say. In angry response Pritchett jerked her to him and lowered his toothy mouth to hers. She was pulling away even as his other hand reached up to grab hold of her tightly coiled braid; she could feel his fingernails digging into her scalp. In spite of all her best efforts, his mouth ground against hers. *How dare you?* she thought, rage such as she had never known flowing through her.

Pritchett wrapped his arms around her struggling body, forcing her back against her service vehicle, leaning against her with the strength of his legs. She was pinned there, helpless. His mouth was still on hers, and his cheek was pressing against her nostril. She made little moaning sounds as she tried to breathe, and her rage began to turn to the sickening nausea of fear. Where was Giff? she thought. No matter what had passed between them just now, surely he would never allow an employee to maul her like this.

Pritchett raised his head at last, his eyes glittering at her evilly. She felt the violating hardness of his body against her clothing and thought, will I be raped here in the parking lot?

She was almost unbelieving when he released her, sauntering away with a terrifying nonchalance. She watched him walk toward his own vehicle and turned dazed eyes from him to glance quickly at the office window where Giff could have seen everything clearly. But Giff was studiously looking down at his paperwork, and in her confusion she supposed it was possible he had seen nothing. She did not want to think that he had seen Bob Pritchett misuse her so and not rushed to her rescue. She did not want to believe that Giff hated her that much.

Yet a silent voice whispered, *Giff saw. He saw, and did nothing.*

Later, she would try to remember the individual activities of that day, but she could not. The only thing that stood out with vivid clarity was the job she had done for the Henrys, another one of Giff's charity cases. The elderly couple, who were completely dependent on their social security checks for their daily sustenance, had been effusive in their gratitude when she refused to leave them a bill.

"Tell Giff thank you," Mr. Henry had said.

"Your uncle is one of the kindest men I know," his aged wife had added.

Giff, the good guy, the hero. No wonder it had taken her so long to see the truth, to feel his betrayal. Even now she was paying the price for her stubborn blindness. She had for too long laid her honesty on the altar of his arrogance, her self-confidence sacrificed too often to appease the guilt he instilled in her.

In the middle of the night she awoke, wet with perspiration, shivering uncontrollably. She barely made it to the bathroom in time to be horribly sick. When she was done, she looked at herself in the mirror and asked herself bitterly why she was still there. She had tried to deal honorably with Giff, but he had made a mockery of her honor. The next four weeks were going to be sheer hell.

A stubborn streak she didn't know she had told her to stay, to endure, to outlast anything Giff could say or do. But every time she thought of what had happened in the parking lot with Bob Pritchett, she gave an inward shudder. It could happen again, she thought, and Giff would not raise a finger to stop it.

Sometimes it takes courage to run.

She went to her closet: her new clothes could easily fit into one suitcase. It was that relatively unimportant fact that helped her reach the decision to leave immediately. It was so easy to bring down her Pullman from the top shelf and open it up. It was unbelievably simple to fold her things and pat them gently into place. The deed was done almost before she had a chance to realize what she was doing, a choice made quickly out of the silent desperation of her soul. Like a thief in the night, she stole soundlessly out of Giff's dark house, a single suitcase in one hand and a grinning, ragged doll in the other. Acting more from instinct than conscious thought, she pointed the hood of her pickup in the direction of Joshua Carter's home. Like a wind-tossed sailor sighting land at last, she was seeking a shelter in the storm.

She rang the bell three times before Joshua came to the door. He was dressed in the same blue and silver robe she had wrapped herself in only yesterday. He took one look at her face and pulled her inside.

"I've left Giff," she told him baldly.

A light flared in his eyes, hard, bright, and triumphant. "Good," he said.

She thought about that as he seated her in one of the kitchen chairs they had purchased together. His movements were quick and sure as he hung up her coat, put on a pot for tea, brushed his hand against her hair.

She felt many things, but *good* was not one of them. She felt confused, scared, hurt. She had just walked out on the only job she had ever known, left behind her the only family she had ever known, and she was bruised and frightened and unsettled. She wondered that he sounded so calm, so confident in his ability to easily label her experience.

He brought her the tea, then pulled up the chair beside her. "I'm proud of you," he said softly. "I never thought you would have the courage so soon."

She looked at him blankly, remembering her nausea and fear. "I had no courage," she said.

Sensing her mood, he fell silent. As the quiet stretched between them, she began to doubt her wisdom in coming here.

Joshua rose in an abruptly impatient movement, scraping the chair legs against the tile on the floor. She felt his hands on her shoulders. They rested there possessively, with new confidence. Those hands sent an unmistakable message: You are mine now.

She stirred uneasily, and after a moment he moved away.

"Talk to me, Jeri," he commanded softly. "Tell me what happened."

She attempted to sip her tea, trying not to notice that her hand was unsteady. I have not stopped shaking for days, she thought. I am in a kaleidoscope, and I don't know yet in which pattern I will fall.

Joshua was waiting expectantly, watching her from where he leaned against the counter. Because she didn't know what else to do, she began to tell him what had occurred since she had left him early Monday morning. She found that when she started, she could hold nothing back, even though the telling brought her shame. She told him about Bob Pritchett with her face averted, afraid she would read disgust in his eyes if she dared to look there.

"Jeri," he said.

She raised wary eyes to his face and saw an expression so unbelievably tender, so full of compassion, that she found it hard to understand the resentment that welled in her like a great angry tide. She tried to tamp it down, tried to tell herself she was in the throes of unreasonable reaction, tried to smile at this man who was standing there watching her with such loving eyes.

"Don't look at me like that," she blurted out at last, her voice ragged with an anger that came from a place deep and dark inside her. "You love me too much, Joshua."

He raised one of his beautiful eyebrows in gentle amusement as his mouth quirked upward. She knew she had failed to make him understand. She hardly understood, herself. Why am I here? she asked herself wearily. I don't love this man. I just love for him to love me. It's a new experience, having someone love me. But I don't love him in return. I don't love anybody.

But the pleasure of being loved was still there, despite her newfound honesty. There was joy to be had sitting here in Joshua's kitchen, sipping his tea, having him care for her. There was a certain enchantment in being comforted and coddled and treasured. She found she actually wanted Joshua to tell her again how beautiful she was, how brave and strong and fine. She could pretend she believed him, for a while.

He spoke none of those words, however. He merely held out his hand to her. "Come," he said. "You're tired. We'll settle everything in the morning."

Suddenly, a roaring sounded in her ears, a heavy throbbing began in her veins. "You mean you will settle everything," she said, hearing with Joshua the coldness in her own voice.

His hand dropped back to his side, but the casualness of his stance did not change. "We will settle things together," he corrected. "You're tired, Jeri. Come to bed now."

"No," she said.

That stopped him. She saw his eyes narrow as he eyed her carefully, and she knew he was regarding her as a problem to solve. "No to what?" he asked, his voice suddenly low and very even.

She answered him with a question of her own. "What exactly needs to be settled, Joshua?"

"You need to be settled, in bed," he replied, trying to pacify her with the lightness of his tone. "Now is not the time for a serious discussion, Jeri."

He was probably right, but some fierce compulsion was driving her, filling her with a need to say what must be said, now. If she waited she might agree to the unpardonable, she might tell him the unforgivable. For if she told him she loved him, it would surely be a lie. And he had asked her to marry him, twice. If he asked again, and she accepted, she would cheat him forever. She would not, could not, have Joshua Carter on her conscience. Now was the time to tell him so.

"I don't think I will come up to bed," she said, striving for calm in her tone. "And I don't think we will settle anything in the morning." She stood. Feeling strangely unsteady, she put a hand down on the table for support. "I should not have come here, Joshua. I won't stay." She repeated her words of a moment ago. "You love me too much, Joshua."

He said nothing, merely watched while she tried not to squirm under his even regard.

"I'm sorry for waking you up," she said. "I'm going to leave now."

"Still scared, aren't you, Adams?"

She stared at him, and cold was reflected in her emerald eyes, and ice was filling her heart. "Yes," she whispered, "and no. You wanted me to choose, Joshua. You wanted me to learn to make my own decisions. I can't come straight from Giff to you. I can't do that. Then I will never know who I am.''

"You have a point," he said softly, and once again his eyes became seductive with understanding.

She had not expected his agreement, or the terror that would fill her as a result. She was silent for a moment, wishing he would be angry, that he would give her an excuse to break things between them cleanly, forever. She could feel the rage building in her once again. Fearing it, she said stiffly, "I'll get my coat.''

"Where will you go?''

She made a vague gesture. "Anywhere," she said. "I will be all right.''

"You have nowhere else to go, Jeri," he said, and even though it was true, it enraged her to hear him say it. She heard an echo of his old arrogance as he continued with calm assurance, "Tonight you will stay with me. Tomorrow you can leave, if you still want to.''

She thought of sleeping with him again, of the way his hands would move against her body in the night, of the way her own response would surge, until she would die from wanting him. She would be ready to promise him anything, in the morning.

"I won't stay here," she said bitterly.

She saw his head fly back, as if she had struck him. The beginnings of a fine desperation began in the corners of his eyes.

She turned to go, only to find his hand on her shoulder, whipping her around to face him. "I won't let you go," he said, his eyes flames of fire. "You belong to me. I love you. I want to marry you. I won't let you go off wounded and bleeding like this, to lick your wounds like an animal, alone and isolated from everyone who cares about you.''

She felt burned where he touched her. She felt consumed when he looked at her. And she felt terrified of the knowledge that ran like white heat through his words. "Let go of me, Joshua Carter!" she cried. "I belong to no one!"

Still his hand gripped her shoulder. He brought his other hand to cup her face, and his touch was hard and sure. "Jeri, stay the night. Please."

"Why?" she demanded, her voice a low throb of pain. "So you can convince me that your way is the best way, the only way? Well, I'm not sure it is, Joshua."

She took a shaking breath, then another. She held out her hands to him. "Look at these," she commanded him. "Look at my hands, Joshua. They are not changed at all. They are still bruised and stained and damaged. Just like me, Joshua. I'm the same way. You've talked to me of healing. Well, maybe I need to be alone to heal. Maybe I need to be free of you to choose. I'm sorry I came here, Joshua. Let me go, now."

"You are lying if you tell yourself you haven't changed. When will you quit denying yourself, Jeri?"

"I speak the truth. I deny nothing." Desperation colored her tone.

Suddenly the hand on her shoulder tightened, the fingers on her face tensed. Joshua's eyes burned into hers, before he lowered his head, and she knew with a sense of helplessness that he was going to kiss her. This time his lips were not tender, nor tentative, nor kind. Her resistance was shamefully short, and then she was kissing him back, hungrily, greedily, her hands moving up to pull his head closer, her body curving into his with fiery abandonment.

He pulled himself away, his breath coming in rough gasps against her skin. "You've changed," he said. "Your walls are all gone, and you're scared, but you're mine, Jeri. You belong to me."

"No!" she cried. "I belong to no one, least of all you." She whirled out of his grasp, then turned to face him, filling her lungs with a huge, shuddering breath. Words came tumbling out of her mouth: hot, angry, bitter words that tore down whatever had been built between them. "You destroyed my walls, all right, Joshua," she said. "You wanted to do it and you did. But what have you built in their place? I am nothing now. I feel nothing, I know nothing, I exist in a vacuum. But before that night at Bill's Tavern, I knew who I was. I could deal with my life before you interfered. It wasn't Bob Pritchett who drove me away from Giff's. It wasn't even Giff himself. It was you, Joshua! So tell me how happy you are I've left Giff's. Tell me that we'll settle things together. There is no *together*, Joshua." She laughed raggedly. "You've ravaged me, Joshua Carter. How can I ever love you? To love you would be the same as loving my own destroyer."

Joshua was standing rigid, the warmth in his blue eyes long since grown cold and hard. His hands were knotted at his side, his mouth a thin, grim line.

"I'm going to leave now," she said, knowing she had said enough. "Please don't try to stop me."

And then she left him, walking alone through the corridors of the house, letting herself out his door, trying not to see the bleak emptiness in his eyes as he had watched her leave.

She got back in her pickup and drove out into the road. She had no idea where to go. After miles of aimless driving, she found herself back at the top of Giff's driveway.

Almost without thinking, she parked the pickup on the road and swung herself out of it. She went down the driveway, past Giff's office, past his house, and down to the summer boathouse, closed up now for the season.

Here, years ago, in the ageless beauty of the ancient lake, she had come for healing from her childhood loneliness, her separateness. And it was here she came now, uncaring of the February cold, of the frozen stretches of ice, of the night-white landscape. She stood at the site of all her dreams and hopes and felt a drop of moisture freeze on her cheek. She felt another, then another, and knew that she was crying at last.

What have I done? she cried to the silent stars. What terrible words have I spoken? What awful deed have I accomplished? What madness caused me to tear out my heart and throw it away? For he will never love me now, not ever again. I am the destroyer, not Joshua. I have destroyed everything.

She threw back the hood of her coat and raised her hands to the sky. Out of her throat came a sort of croak, then a groan, followed at last by a long animal howl of grief and pain.

And so she stood, her unbound hair flying in the wind, her hands and face held high, tears freezing as they streamed out of her eyes, and spoke in wordless communication with the stars of the death of all her dreams.

Chapter Ten

Jeri awoke to the comforting scent of fresh-brewed coffee. Raising her head slightly, she opened stiff, puffy eyes, her gaze traveling around the room as she recognized the homely, eclectic furnishings of Susan McDougall's house. She was lying on Susan's second-generation sofa, covered with a thick blanket. An exploratory movement of her hand reminded her that she was stripped to her underwear.

"Susan?" Her throat was raw and tight, making her voice sound like rasping sandpaper. She cleared it painfully, then tried again. "Susan?"

"Right here, honey," came the quick, reassuring response. Susan followed her words by appearing in the kitchen doorway. "I didn't mean to wake you, but I do have to go to work."

Jeri attempted a smile. "Second day on your new job?" she managed roughly.

The redhead nodded, her riot of red curls tamed for the moment in a deceptively simple style.

"What time is it?" Jeri asked, whispering around the soreness in her throat.

"A little after nine. I'll be out of here in fifteen minutes. You just lie back and rest."

That thought had an absolutely heavenly sound to it. Not to have to think, or to do anything at all seemed the most wonderful idea in the world.

"Are you sure you don't mind having me here?" she forced herself to ask.

"You are absolutely welcome, Jeri," Susan assured her, not trying to hide her concern as she examined Jeri's face.

I must look a fright to put that concern in Susan's eyes, Jeri thought.

"Mike won't be back until Friday night," Susan continued with deliberate casualness, "and I could sure use some company."

Jeri's head fell back on the pillow Susan had provided. "Thanks," she said gruffly, tears gathering in her eyes.

"Aw, Jeri," Susan said, moving swiftly to sit on the sofa beside her. "It's my pleasure, honey. You know that. But what happened to you? You had me half petrified when you started knocking on my door at five this morning."

"I suppose I was quite...dramatic," Jeri said, blushing painfully.

"You were desperate," Susan said bluntly. "Do you want to tell me about it, Jeri?"

Jeri shook her head, her eyes sliding away from Susan's uneasily.

"All right, then," Susan agreed, her voice soft and undemanding. "I'll call Joshua for you and let him know where you are."

"No!" Jeri brought her hand up to rest on Susan's arm. She tried to gentle her tone. "No, please."

Susan looked at her, openly puzzled. Jeri attempted an explanation. "I saw Joshua before I came to you. I . . . we . . . he won't want to talk with me. He won't care where I am now."

"I think we should let Joshua make up his own mind about that, don't you think?" Susan asked mildly.

But Jeri was adamant. She would leave now if Susan called Joshua. She did not want to see the blond-haired builder. She did not want to speak with him. She did not want him to know where she was.

In the end, Susan merely shrugged.

After Susan left, Jeri fell into a sleep so deep that when she awoke she had a terrifying sense of complete disorientation. For a moment she lay quietly, her eyes on Susan's ceiling, with no recollection of why she was here, or what had gone before. I must have been very ill, was her first disjointed thought before memory came rushing back, causing her to moan slightly. She closed her eyes against its potent force and lay that way for some time before she heard the door to the house opening and knew she had slept the day away. Susan was home.

Jeri spoke very little that evening. Susan, however, felt no such reticence as she said, while tearing lettuce for a salad, "Bob Pritchett left town today."

Jeri's hands stilled over the carrots she was shredding. "What did you say?" she asked.

Susan sighed. "You might as well know, Jeri. The talk is all over town. Pritchett was having lunch today at the little diner on Clark Street when Joshua walked in. Joshua had spent the morning looking for him, and he was in a pretty determined mood. They shared some strong words, Jeri, and your name was mentioned more than once. One thing led to another, and they . . . fought." Susan's head was bowed over the salad bowl. "Whatever Pritchett did to you, Jeri, he won't be around to do it again."

Jeri's face had gone white, all color drained from it as she asked in a small, strained voice, "And Joshua? Was he hurt?"

Susan looked up, directly into Jeri's green eyes. "I went to see him after work. He's got a black eye, and he had to have stitches in his chin. But my understanding is Pritchett looked a heck of a lot worse. And the word is, Pritchett is already gone." Susan ripped a last piece of lettuce, once again staring down at her hands. "Joshua wants to see you."

That took a moment to sink in. "You told him I was here," Jeri said.

Susan shrugged, still looking at the salad. "He was worried. It seemed cruel to say nothing."

He was worried. Three small words that opened the floodgates to feelings she had buried deep in her heart. She had told him she didn't love him. She had said other things, too. In her desperate fear she had used harsh, ugly words that could never be forgotten, or forgiven.

"You love him, don't you?" Susan asked quietly.

Maybe I do, she thought. *If I were capable of loving anyone, I would certainly love Joshua Carter.*

"I don't know," she whispered. "I am so confused."

"Will you see him?"

Panic shot through her. "No," she murmured. "Not yet."

That night as she lay trying to sleep on Susan's sofa, she thought of Giff, who was now suddenly missing two employees. He would be doubly furious, she acknowledged, and then thought: how curious. Giff's problems don't bother me at all. He is simply no longer my concern. And then she wondered, is this how it feels to be free?

Over breakfast the next morning Susan asked, "What are your plans, Jeri?"

She thought carefully before responding. "I need to find an apartment, probably in Traverse City or Charlevoix." She had named the two largest towns with which she was familiar. "I have to get another job. But the only thing I know how to do is fix furnaces, and I'm not sure I want to do that anymore."

"Why don't you go to school?" Susan suggested. "From what you've told me, you've saved enough money to last you a good long time, indeed. Traverse City has a junior college. It's supposed to be one of the best in the state. You could start there."

"I'd never thought of it," Jeri replied. "But I suppose that's a possibility."

My life is full of unexpected possibilities and new beginnings, she thought. Suddenly everything can be conceived; there is nothing that is not allowed.

Even loving, and being loved.

Later, as she helped Susan clean and straighten the small living room, she asked hesitantly. "How long have you known Joshua, Susan?"

"Why, as long as I have known Mike, which is about ten years, I guess."

"Then you must have known Helen," Jeri commented.

Susan puffed up a throw pillow and tossed it lightly against the sofa arm. "Yes, I knew her," she admitted.

"Joshua said she was very beautiful."

Susan laughed lightly. "She was. You always imagined her in the pages of some glossy magazine, being one of the beautiful people, you know? But that was just about all she had going for her. She was the shallowest person I have ever known."

Susan sat down in an easy chair and eyed Jeri carefully. "You have no reason to be jealous of Helen," she said, causing Jeri to flush slightly, remembering when Joshua had said those same words. "Helen was terribly self-centered, and my Mike couldn't stand her. He tried to hide his feelings for Joshua's sake, but Helen knew how he felt. Once, when she was alone with Mike, she taunted him, saying that after she and Joshua married, he would no longer be welcome as Joshua's friend. But that wasn't the worst."

Jeri waited, picking an imaginary speck of dust off of Susan's sofa.

"Helen used to come on to Mike whenever Joshua wasn't around. Mike would just laugh at her, but it bothered him a lot. He used to tell me that if Joshua really did marry Helen, he didn't see how they could maintain their relationship. It was tearing him apart, because he and Joshua have always been like brothers."

"If she was as bad as you say, what did Joshua see in her?"

"He'd been smitten for years, and she was really a pretty potent force when she wanted to be. She could turn on the charm and make a man feel as if he were the only person in the room worth talking to. And Joshua is such a dreamboat, I think she carried around this picture in her head of what they looked like when they were together. She was constantly posing at his side, as if she expected someone to be snapping photographs."

"She hurt him badly," Jeri said flatly. *And so did I. Joshua Carter is singularly unfortunate in his choice of women.*

"You're telling me. Mike watched over him pretty carefully when Helen finally left him. When Joshua eventually recovered, he was a changed man."

"Oh? How?"

"It's hard to put into words, exactly. More careful, I think. More deliberate. More sensitive to other people's pain. Much more caring." Susan paused, then met Jeri's eyes as she said with slow deliberation, "He's been a great friend to us, and I have learned to love him just as much as Mike does. You could do a lot worse than Joshua Carter, Jeri."

Jeri had plenty of time to think about those words after Susan had left for work. She wandered about Susan's little house aimlessly, until finally restlessness drove her out into her truck. She spent the afternoon hunting for apartments in Traverse City, and by the end of the day she had signed for one. It was neither particularly classy nor full of character, but it was hers. She returned to Susan's brimming with enthusiasm.

Susan smiling, listened to Jeri's description of her new home. "That's great," she said, when Jeri finished. "Obviously finding a place of your own was very important to you."

It was important, Jeri told herself firmly. And she had managed to spend almost four whole hours without once thinking of Joshua Carter. That was a sort of milestone, too.

But later, in the silence of the little house, she could not drive him from her mind. Things that he had said, little nuances that were his own peculiarities, kept haunting her in the night. And she remembered over and over her last words to him: *I could never love you. You are my destroyer.*

Thursday she went to the college, discovering enrollment procedures, thinking about her future. She found herself phrasing questions to Joshua in her mind. *What do you think of this class?* she wanted to ask him. *Do you think I would enjoy Art 101?*

She wanted to tell him about her apartment. *Of course, it's nothing like your house. It's pretty simple really, only one bedroom. I can almost see the bay from the living-room window. And the lease I signed was only for six months...*

Thursday evening when Susan got home from work Jeri had already made dinner. "Smells good," the redhead said gratefully. "You're looking better, too," she added, eyeing Jeri critically.

Jeri watched Susan hang up her coat, feeling a rush of tenderness for this new friend who had welcomed her so easily in her home. Susan bent to unzip her boots. "Joshua came by the store today," she remarked casually.

Jeri stiffened. "Oh?"

"He sure has one heck of a multicolored eye."

"I see."

"Yes, well—" Susan turned to her, an impish light in her brown eyes, "—I thought you might be interested."

"Did he . . . did he ask about me?"

"Not this time, honey," Susan said gently. Then, seeing the stark unhappiness in Jeri's expression, she relented. "He didn't have to. I knew why he came around. I told him you were doing better." Susan walked into the kitchen. "I told him you got an apartment, too."

"You did? What did he say to that?"

"Nothing much. He just sort of went all still and expressionless, you know what I mean?" Susan paused. "I wish you would go see that man, Jeri. He needs to be put out of his misery."

Jeri's eyes flooded with tears. In an instant Susan was beside her, holding her, crooning in her ear. "I said such terrible things to him, Susan," Jeri choked. "Really awful things. And I left him, when he wanted me to stay. How can he possibly want to see me ever again?"

"I don't know, honey. But he wants to see you. That man is hurting, and you're the only medicine that will work."

"I'm scared, Susan. I want to tell him I'm sorry, it's all I can think about, but what if he laughs at me, or tells me that it wasn't important?"

"He won't laugh, Jeri."

She took a deep breath then. She remembered standing outside the door of Bill's Tavern, Susan by her side. She had overcome that terror; she would overcome this.

"Tomorrow is Friday," she said. "I . . . we'd planned on spending Fridays together, decorating his house. I'll go then."

"Good." Susan grinned. "Now, let's eat this wonderful dinner. I find I'm absolutely ravenous."

Friday morning Jeri dressed slowly, choosing her purple pants and lavender shirt. A thousand butterflies had made their home in her stomach, and she decided at least three times not to go to Joshua's after all. In the end it was her need to see him, one last time, that pulled her with almost magnetic force to the door of his home.

She tried the door when she arrived at Joshua's: it was unlocked. Quietly she let herself inside. Slipping off her shoes, she moved on stockinged feet through the silent house, gliding up the stairs and down the hallway until she reached the door to Joshua's room.

It was slightly ajar, and she could see him plainly through the narrow space. Like a peeping tom, she gazed at him as he sat at his table, papers spread untidily as he worked.

A rush of tenderness swept through her, and for a moment she was still. Yes, she thought. It is good to feel so when I see you. She watched Joshua run his hand through his hair, and he turned slightly, so that she saw for the first time the brilliant purples and greens around his left eye. She saw a vivid red slash across the left side of his chin, with stitches plainly marked. Involuntarily she gasped.

She saw Joshua's back go rigid as his hands stilled upon his work. She saw his head come up, the veins in his neck suddenly taut and prominent.

"Joshua?" she said.

He turned to face her, and she was sure she had not mistaken the leaping, glad light in his eyes before he shuttered them closed. She opened the door farther and took a step inside his room, her hand outstretched in involuntary supplication. But when he looked at her again, his eyes were cold and hard, and she found herself swallowing uncomfortably, her hand dropping impotently to her side.

"Hello, Joshua," she said.

"Jeraldine." He inclined his head briefly.

"May I come in?"

His mouth quirked at that, in a gesture so familiar she felt tears gather behind her lids. "You're already in, Jeri."

"May I . . . may I sit down?"

"Suit yourself." He turned from her back to his work. Biting her lip, she moved to sit in one of the wing chairs by the fireplace. She could afford to be patient. She would wait.

He worked for perhaps a quarter of an hour more before he finally threw down his pencil and looked at her, sighing. "Why are you here, Jeraldine?" he asked. His voice was gentle and kind, and absolutely impersonal. It terrified her.

His eyes rested on her hands, which were twisting themselves nervously in the folds of her sweater. She willed them to be still, even as she forced her eyes to meet his evenly. "I've come to . . . to apologize, Joshua," she managed.

"Oh?"

"Yes. The things I said the other night, about you . . .

about you destroying...' The words stuck in her throat, she felt her face go a bright red. She found she could not repeat the harsh, ugly words, but doggedly she continued, saying instead, "I said a lot of very stupid things. You were right when you said I was not myself. What I said and what I did to you by coming to you Monday night was unpardonable. I am deeply ashamed, and I wanted you know I was sorry."

Joshua rose from his chair and walked to where she was sitting. For a moment he stood over her, looking at her broodingly. She forced herself not to turn away from his searching gaze. She looked for some sign of affection in his eyes but could find none. She thought with sudden desolation, I really did destroy any feeling he had for me. I really did kill his love.

Joshua took the wing chair opposite her. "Very prettily said," he murmured, never taking his eyes from her.

At least he had not asked her to leave. There were still other things that needed to be said. "I heard from Susan where you got that...that shiner, Joshua. I...want to thank you for fighting Pritchett for me." That was especially hard to get out and sounded unbelievably stiff. She was not surprised when Joshua laughed harshly.

"You're welcome, I think."

She did look away then as she stared with seeming fascination at the cold fireplace. "Does it...does it hurt very much?"

"Not too much. Not very much at all now that you're here."

The words, spoken so softly, with such tender gentleness, took a moment to register in her mind.

She clasped her hands in her lap, only to be twisting them around each other seconds later.

"Are you ready to admit you love me, just a little, Jeri?"

Her eyes flew back to his, unbelieving of the joy and re-lief that washed over her in a baptism of happiness. "Joshua?" she asked, and her whole heart was laid bare before him with the simple question.

"Come over here, Jeri. Let me touch you."

Unquestioning, she rose from her chair and went to his, where she stood looking at him. His eye was swollen and bruised, his chin sore and red. Yet he had never looked so beautiful to her as he did at this moment. His arms came up, beckoning her, and she lowered herself so that she was on his lap. She felt his arms surround her. She raised her face to his, and his lips came down on hers in a kiss of exquisite sweetness, telling her of sorrow, of forgiveness, of love. She put her arms around his chest and leaned against him. "I am so sorry," she said.

"Ah, Jeri," he said. "That's one of the things I love about you most. You are one of the most sincerely honest people I have ever met."

"Do you love me?" she asked. "I've never understood how you could."

"Shall I explain it to you?"

"Yes, please," she said, trusting that he would not mis-take her very real need to understand for anything less than it was.

He shifted in the chair, so that she fit easily into him. Her hand rested against his shoulder; he grasped her hand and twisted it against his chest in a gesture that bespoke of a new intimacy between them.

"Shall I tell you of your beauty?" he asked, almost teas-ingly. "You have always been lovely and so unaware of it. I would find any excuse I could just to talk to you, to see your eyes flash and smoulder, to watch your lips curve in the most natural smile I'd ever seen.

"But there was pain there, too. You had known hurt and rejection and suffering, and you were strong because of it. Because you knew these things, I felt I could trust you. I have learned that someone who understands suffering does not belittle the pain of another.

"You were intelligent and resourceful. That was obvious in the quality of the work you did every day, but you really bowled me over when I saw what you had done with Giff's house.

"And you are honest. I had never heard you purpose-fully lie, even to yourself, or try to cheat a customer, or deal falsely with anyone, man or woman.

"At first I just watched you and took pleasure in it. And then I learned to love you. You are no illusion for me, Jeri. I knew just what I was going for when I wanted you. You are a woman of grace, of courage, of rare intelligence and integrity. But you were asleep, blind to your own attri-butes. I vowed I would be the one who was next to you when your eyes were opened. Are they open now, Jeri?"

She was crying softly as he said, "I love you, Jeri Adams. If it takes the rest of my life, I'll hear the words from you, too."

Gently he stroked her back as her tears wet his shirt front. She felt his strength surround her, his love envelop her. "Will you give me time?" she asked humbly.

"All the time in the world," he answered gravely.

"I am so afraid."

"Love will overcome your fear."

"Will you kiss me now?"

"As many times as you like."

Sometime later she said, "Susan told you about my apartment."

"Yes."

"The lease is for six months."

"That's good. We'll have plenty of time to plan our wedding. Maybe my house will even be furnished by then."

She laughed then, as full of joy and peace and hope as she knew how to be. "Maybe it will," she said. "But if not, we will have the rest of our lives to finish it."

"Yes." The single word stretched out on a sigh of contentment. It was at that moment in the quiet of the winter morning, feeling herself loved beyond anything she could ever have imagined, that she gathered her strength about her. For a final word had yet to be said.

"Joshua?"

"Hmmm?"

"I . . . I do love you." It is no lie, she thought. Only the truth could bring with it such peace.

A slight pause, a short, husky laugh.

"I know it, babe. I always have. I was just waiting for you to find out, too."

Somewhere, in a place heard only by the heart, a battle was won, a final wall crumbled. But there was no desolation in the eyes of the vanquished, and the song of the victor was wisdom and truth and love.

Jeraldine Adams was home at last.

* * * * *

Bestselling author **NORA ROBERTS** captures all the romance, adventure, passion and excitement of Silhouette in a special miniseries.

THE CALHOUN WOMEN

Four charming, beautiful and fiercely independent sisters set out on a search for a missing family heirloom—an emerald necklace—and each finds something even more precious...passionate romance.

Look for THE CALHOUN WOMEN miniseries starting in June.

COURTING CATHERINE
in Silhouette Romance #801 (June/$2.50)

A MAN FOR AMANDA
in Silhouette Desire #649 (July/$2.75)

FOR THE LOVE OF LILAH
in Silhouette Special Edition #685 (August/$3.25)

SUZANNA'S SURRENDER
in Silhouette Intimate Moments #397 (September/$3.25)

Available at your favorite retail outlet, or order any missed titles by sending your name, address, zip or postal code along with a check or money order (please do not send cash) for the price as shown above, plus 75¢ postage and handling ($1.00 in Canada) payable to Silhouette Reader Service to:

In the U.S.	In Canada
3010 Walden Ave.	P.O. Box 609
P.O. Box 1396	Fort Erie, Ontario
Buffalo, NY 14269-1396	L2A 5X3

Please specify book title(s) with your order.
Canadian residents add applicable federal and provincial taxes.   CALWOM-2

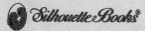 *Silhouette Books®*

PUT SOME SIZZLE INTO YOUR SUMMER WITH

SILHOUETTE
SUMMER

1991

Heading your way this summer are three sensual and
romantic stories by these award-winning authors:

Kathleen Eagle
Marilyn Pappano
Patricia Gardner Evans

Sit back, bask in the sun and celebrate summer with
this special collection of stories about three college
roommates who rekindle their friendship—and
discover love.

Available in June at your favorite retail outlets.

SIZZ

Take 4 bestselling love stories FREE

Plus get a FREE surprise gift!

A Lasting Love

The passionate Cancer man is destined for love this July in Val Whisenand's FOR ETERNITY, the latest in our compelling WRITTEN IN THE STARS series.

Sexy Adam Gaines couldn't explain the eerie sense of familiarity that arose each time his eyes met Kate Faraday's. But Mexico's steamy jungles were giving the star-crossed lovers another chance to make their love last for all eternity....

FOR ETERNITY by Val Whisenand is coming this July from Silhouette Romance. It's WRITTEN IN THE STARS!

Silhouette Romance®

JULYSTAR